First published in Great Britain in 2006 by Comma Press
3rd Floor, 24 Lever Street, Manchester M1 1DW
www.commapress.co.uk

'A Man of the Streets' was first published as 'Un homme des rues' in *La Liberté des Rues* (Gallimard, 1997). 'The First Day of the Fourth Week' was first published as 'Fyrsti dagur fjórðu viku' in *Tvisvar á ævinni* (Skrudda, 2004). 'The Inferior Quality of Contemporary Poetry' first appeared as 'La baixa qualitat de la poesia contemporánia' in *Testimo si he begut* (Quaderns Crema, 2004). 'The Carnage on Via Palestro', 'Yoghurt' and 'Argentina Brasile Africa' first appeared as *La strage di via Palestro*, 'Lo yogurt' and 'Argentina Brasile Africa' in *Superwoobinda* (Einaudi, 1998). 'Once in a lifetime...' first appeared as 'Samo jednom se, ono, a poslje ga moš forgetit / Popizditis mijelitis / Univerzijada' in *Kavice Andreja Puplina* (Durieux, 2002). 'The Four Hundred Pleats' was first published in Greece as 'Tetrakosies pietes' in *Me opthanioxta matia* (Kastaniotis, 2004), edited by Katerina Fragou. 'The News and Views' first appeared as 'Události a komentáre' in *O Létajících Objektech* (Argo, 2004). 'Something for Nothing' was first published as 'Zaungäste' in *Schwalbensommer* (Eichborn, 2003). And 'My Mother's Men' first appeared as 'De mannen van mijn moeder' in *Amuse-Gueule* (Nijgh & Van Ditmar, 2001).

A CIP catalogue record of this book is available from the British Library

ISBN: 1 905583 03 6
EAN: 978 1 905583 03 4

The publishers gratefully acknowledge assistance from the Arts Council England North West, and the following institutions who have helped with the launch events for this book: Instituto Cervantes, the Goethe Institut Manchester, the Hellenic Foundation for Culture as part of Greece in Britain 2006, Icelandair, the University of Bolton, and GMPTE (Greater Manchester Public Transport Executive).

Set in Bembo by XL Publishing Services, Tiverton
Printed and bound in England by SRP Ltd, Exeter.

DECAPOLIS

TALES FROM TEN CITIES

EDITED BY
MARIA CROSSAN

CONTENTS

CONTENTS

Introduction:
Writing the City

> Writing the city is not the same as writing about
> the city. The former transforms and translates...
> *Julian Wolfreys*

Do you know your city? How many versions of our own city do we negotiate, day-to-day, to arrive at our sense of it as a space? The city we work in is not the same city we play in, and not the same city that others come to visit; the city where we are born is, for people who migrate there, another space entirely; the routes by which we walk our cities are rarely the routes the town planners intended us to take. Our cities are spaces ordered by infinitely different mechanisms — chance, choice, function — according to who experiences them, and how. There is not a single Manchester, nor one Athens, nor one Prague, but thousands upon thousands of individual cities moving within their boundaries. And they don't ever sit still. Spatial theorist Michel de Certeau argued that, in our everyday manipulations of physical city-space, city dwellers 'create in the planned city a "metaphorical" city, or a city in movement,' with the different versions of this city clashing and fusing, overlapping and intersecting constantly. How do we, and moreover how can writing, then, come to terms with this multiplicity and movement inherent in the city?

The idea of *Tales from ten cities* – an anthology of stories from ten cities, with the stories from nine translated into English here for the first time – already sounds problematic. How can an anthology possibly justify the juxtaposition of a city's name with just one story, as if it could give you the means to 'know' a city, a single city, in two or three thousand words? Let alone go on to repeat this conceit ten times, as though we could seriously claim to offer, hidebound between the covers of this book, an encyclopaedic knowledge of all the ten cities that make an appearance here. It's almost an invitation to make sweeping statements about 'the European city' in general. It all begins to feel slightly disingenuous...

And what of that third layer of this book's conceit, translation itself? If 'the literary' or 'the poetic' might be defined as that which cannot truly be paraphrased in its own language, the translation of a literary work directly and unproblematically out of the original language and straight into another without movement or slippage must be regarded as an impossible task. Even when the stories wear their translated nature lightly, knowingly, there is still a deceit: Empar Moliner's fictional poet, Susaeta bemoans the French translation of his poem for its lack of 'strength' compared to the original. And yet it is an English translation from the Catalan, that here masquerades as the 'original'.

Add to this the translations of stories which hinge on the faithful rendering of dialects and slang forms unique to finite urban districts – the disjointed, harsh slang of Dalibor Šimpraga's 1990s civil-wartime Zagreb, for example – which, when translated into English, make unavoidable the fact that approximations have to be found, and you have yet another stratum to add to this anthology's project. The architecture of the text that we encounter, as English readers, is necessarily to a greater or lesser degree remote from the original. In other stories here where diction and dialogue present less of an obvious challenge, we are offered an English translation merely studded with exotic foreign street-names and landmarks, but the 'access' to the cities they create can be no more direct. Whether we hope to find in these translations a version of city life which is comfortingly familiar newly-rendered in our own tongue, or an exotic Other to our own urban experience lived out on strange streets, we are assuming that the texts - and the cities they articulate - were entirely at home with themselves *in their original language*, and that they can be rendered exactly into English. The truth is that, in any language, the city is a space where one never feels completely at home, and the slipperiness of language is an intrinsic component of that unhomeliness.

To compound all of this, presenting these city-like experiences in well-crafted literary works adds yet another layer to this book's deceptive veneer; that is, in works which replicate the chance and coincidence of city living in very deliberate narrative structures. In Jacques Réda's Paris-set piece 'A Man of the Streets', for example, the intersection of the two characters' paths which sparks the story is far from coincidental in the author's intentions; it is, rather, a very much orchestrated exercise. Both Dalibor Šimpraga's 'coffee chats', snatched moments of 'overheard' conversations, and Larissa Boehning's fluid, flowing syntax, seemingly given over to the spontaneous nature of city life, are consciously-deployed literary devices. They pin down, on the printed page, what is quicksilver, constantly changing, ultimately ungraspable. Concealed or otherwise, the rub between the city and writing persists: as David Constantine's protagonist has it here, 'there is no liveliness of words comes anywhere near the life of life itself.'

A decidedly precarious construction begins to emerge from these myriad layers of conceit: how can there be justification – given everything that weighs against even the remotest possibility of any success in 'representing' the city – for bringing together these short stories in this format?

The answer, of course, is there in the question: there is and can be no such possibility. The short stories collected here make no such pretensions towards any idea of full representation of their cities or indeed anything else, and this is written into their very form. The short story is not simply any kind of writing. The best short stories are those which admit their partiality and artifice at the outset, and also that the accounts they present are only selections from an infinite number of others. A successful short story does not aspire to completeness, and makes a virtue of the necessarily fragmentary and momentary insight it is able to provide. In Nadine Gordimer's terms, the writer of short fiction (unlike the novelist) is able to remain faithful to what she calls 'the quality of human life, where contact is more like the flash of fireflies, in and out, now here, now there, in darkness. Short-story writers see by the light of the flash.' In not allowing – or indeed aiming – for the novelist's privilege of protracted physical description or their aspirations towards a definitive account, the seemingly unsustainable 'edifice' that is *Decapolis* becomes somehow entirely appropriate. Indeed, it is this very unsustainability that gives an anthology such as this licence for its conceits: if we were to collect hundreds of stories from just one city it would still betray some hope that, by way of some process of adjudication, the definitive story of that city could be pieced together. By taking just one perspective on each city, and thus freely admitting that perspective's non-generalisable nature, the approach of this anthology is paradoxically truer to the multiple spirit of the city.

The city and the short story are in fact apposite bookfellows. The stories collected here can be seen to participate in wider shifts in how city-dwellers are perceived to experience their environments, and even how those environments are themselves constituted. Geographical theory in general is said to have undergone a 'spatial turn' in recent years, in which the Kantian model of space – as an inert container for human action – is rejected in favour of a sense of space 'as process and in process,' as geographers Mike Crang and Nigel Thrift have put it. Spatial theorist Doreen Massey, in her recent manifesto-like *For Space*, calls for a recognition that space, and specific spaces, are constituted by the ever-shifting interrelations of people and of forces. Spaces, for her, are 'never finished, never closed. Perhaps we could imagine space as a simultaneity of stories-so-far.' In the same way that literary theory has long inflected its terminology with the spatial ('structure', 'form', and so on), the writing of space and place has now taken on board the language of literature: 'composition'; 'textuality'; 'stories'.

Massey's simultaneity is a useful concept to get to grips with here, as it brings the city and stories into close correspondence: space, for her, is 'the sphere in which distinct trajectories coexist.' The same can be said of the short fiction. It admits incompleteness rather than strives for a singularity of perspective. Gordimer's assertion that 'each of us has a thousand lives, and the novel gives a character only one,' runs parallel to Massey's criticism of traditional geographical theory's repression of the characteristics of space: it is only capable of allowing spaces such as the city one life, when in reality they have a multiplicity of lives. We arrive, via these works of theory, at a sense of the city as made up of innumerable simultaneous stories, not one story. And, by the same logic, at a sense of the short story as the ideal form in which to express these atomised urban experiences.

In these stories we come across a repeated structural element: the encounter. We tend not to be presented here with stories which take place within pre-formed relationships and structures, but rather are party to the very moment of their formation, the point at which Massey's stories-so-far intersect and fuse into another configuration. It's a textual manoeuvre that seems to transcend all boundaries of context: in these stories people meet on buses, on benches, over second-hand goods, over begged cigarettes. Almost every piece collected here pivots on just such a 'beginning', and it's a fulcrum for narrative that only the city could possibly sustain, and only the short story could possibly express. Where perhaps this conception of city-space could seem to preclude the formation of any meaningful relationships, and to produce an unstable space in which the urban protagonist must remain anonymous, itinerant and detached, here 'the encounter' provides a structuring element that weaves a fabric of connections quite distinct from the familial and social networks of any other form of inhabited space.

A number of the stories here feature variations on the encounter theme, where the protagonist and the 'encountered' character never actually meet: in Larissa Boehning's story, for example, the shared witnessing of the aftermath of an accident – forming just such a 'non-contact' encounter, an accidental intimacy – precipitates another intimacy, between the two central characters. Similarly, in David Constantine's piece, it is the strange lens of the recovery of a drowned man's body from the river that focuses the narrator's reflection on the story's 'central' encounter. These stories continually demonstrate why the encounter is so powerful an experience for their characters, and so powerful a device for the writer of the city: we all crave intimacy in the very non-intimate surroundings of the city, and the encounter represents the desire to sate this need, to find intimacy somewhere, anywhere, even if only for a moment.

The encounter is a narrative element with a pre-programmed time-limit. It crucially imposes only a momentary structure on the story, often breaking up, moving on and (we suppose) reforming elsewhere as quickly as it occurred. In David Constantine's story, we are party to the last time that the narrator and the girl he knows only as 'M' cross paths; similarly, the space that blossoms into being in

Jacques Réda's 'A Man of the Streets' at the coincidence of a businessman's daily ramblings and the rather less august path of Georges Louis, a 'true man of the streets,' dissolves just as quickly as it was formed, all within the confines of the story.

This sense of inevitable change, of stories which span a turning point, animates a number of these pieces. In Larissa Boehning's and Ágúst Borgþór Sverrisson's stories we come across similar experiences, with different resonances: in both, the central characters visit and wander through disused factories, which focuses for both the inexorable pace of change. In Boehning's piece, the abandoned factory, left exactly as it was on the last day of production – 'a nice image' – stands for the abrupt end of a way of life under a certain regime. In Ágúst Borgþór's piece, the central character's mind remains firmly oriented toward the past, and the abandoned factory (where he himself worked) embodies the destructive force that change – both technological and social – represents for him. In both, though, it is the swiftness and unpredictable direction of change that focuses a reflection: where did this all go? In Emil Hakl's story, change flows in the opposite direction: the protagonist finds himself standing on a puzzlingly newly-appeared hill in a district of Prague which, upon further enquiry, he finds has only been there for a year and a half. This sense of constant and unavoidable mutability not only highlights the impossibility of representing a city with a single voice, but that from one moment to the next the city's very physicality never settles into a single version. The city is forever a multiplicity of terrains; David Constantine's Manchester revolves around locations, for example, like Central Station and Telephone House, which a modern-day resident of the city would be hard pressed to locate.

It's a manoeuvre that becomes programmatic in these stories. They revel in the fact that the relationships, spaces and cities they create can only be held in suspension for the space of the narrative. Empar Moliner's mocking take on the folly of city-writing in 'The Inferior Quality of Contemporary Poetry' captures the almost giddy progress towards the inevitable dissolution of these pieces' city-spaces. With each revision of Susaeta's lyric poem we watch the city gradually disappear, breaking up under the weight of the expectation placed on it. In the end, the ridiculous, elliptical fruit of Susaeta's labours does stand as testament to Barcelona, but not in the way that he imagines. In its impenetrability, its obliqueness to its original purpose, and the endless collaborative editing process in which the intention of the writer becomes completely lost, the text does indeed, for a moment, capture something of the experience of experiencing Barcelona – the process of writing the poem, the futile attempt to write the city, becomes the purpose of the story itself.

The sense of an inevitable and constant mutability, the vertiginous feeling of a story perched on a precipice right before the whole thing comes crashing down, inflects most of these pieces (quite literally, in the case of Amanda Michalopoulou's 'The Four Hundred Pleats' and its fevered pace towards the edge). In Emil Hakl's 'The News and Views', the crammed interior of a Prague tram with its disparate groups of passengers and innumerable languages comes to stand in the protagonist's imagination for the city's dizzyingly unsustainable proliferation of narratives; a space so loaded with different stories and different ways of telling them that it collapses – with delirious abandon – under its own weight:

> ...there was talking in Czech, Russian, English, the iron tongues of the North, the wooden ones of the Balkans and the watery ones of the East, there was shouting in German and whispering in Ukrainian and mumbling in Hittite, Chaldean and Aramaic. And there was […] a feeling that all these languages were seamlessly melting together and into one another and

that they were returning to their original state at the time when it was more than enough to grunt, boo, hiss, sputter, howl, and produce inarticulate roaring and all-encompassing laughter.

If ever there were a time in Europe's history to begin to come to terms with the expression of the urban experience, it's now. More than ever before, cities and their authorities are provided with opportunities to represent themselves to the outside world: conferences, conventions, sporting events, summits, as capitals of culture, heritage sites, tourist destinations; opportunities to which they step up with gusto. The world's media descends on a city and expects to be fed a coherent story, branded, with a logo and slogan to match. But, as Empar Moliner's poet discovers – writing his commission for the fictional Worldwide State Leader's Meeting – the city continues to respond in characteristic form: changing, resisting, slipping away. Revising. Editing. Rewriting.

Maria Crossan, Sep 06

MANCHESTER

Beginning

DAVID CONSTANTINE

Coming home from visiting my mother, distressed that she no longer knows who I am and cannot make any sounds that I recognize as words, I set down the odd fact that on this day forty-five years ago, 31 May 1961, coming home from school under blue skies, I saw my first dead fellow human being. He was in the river under Victoria Bridge where I caught my second bus, the 64 or the 66. I was seventeen. I've seen few dead since then, far fewer than the averagely unlucky seven year-old in Gaza or Baghdad has already seen. I had a good look at him. Scores of people were leaning over the parapet and doing the same. I looked and looked. And when I got home I wrote him up in my notebook, that drowned man.

On the first bus, the 42 from Birchfields Road to Albert Square, I sometimes met a girl and we sat together, if we could. Our meetings weren't arranged but they weren't entirely accidental either. I worked out which buses were most likely on which days, and went for those. But once on a bus I had no hope about, nearly an hour later than our usual times, there she was. So really I never knew. We sat upstairs, if there was room, with the smokers. Often it was sunny and the curls, the ringlets, the spiralling, floating, unravelling tresses of bluish smoke in the beams of sun made a pretty effect. I say often, but I don't suppose I saw her more than a dozen times. I never even knew her name. All I know is it began with 'M'. She'd be there already, if it was a lucky day, sitting upstairs in the sunny smoke and saving me a place next to her on the front seat, if we were especially lucky. All we talked about was books, and I never touched her except in the way you are bound to if you sit next to somebody on a bus and you turn and forget yourself in conversation. I remember her eyes, the soul staring out of them, eager and scared, and I remember her lips and tongue but not any single sentence that she said, only the tone, the rhythms, the feel of her speech, so close, the aura of her. She got off a couple of stops before me, near Central Station, and of course I don't know where she went from there. A couple of days before I saw the man in the river she gave me a present, as she was getting off. She took it out of her satchel as she stood up, thrust it at my heart, and was gone. I never saw her again.

I didn't open the girl's present until I was upstairs on the 64 on Victoria Bridge. The buses started from there and you might have to wait a while before they were due to leave. All the years I was going to school, and for many before that, so I am told, there was a madman on Victoria Bridge, called Charlie. He wore the cap and jacket of a sort of uniform and he believed himself to be in charge of the comings and goings of the buses on Victoria Bridge. He had a pocket watch, that he consulted frequently, and a notebook, and one of those pencils you have to keep licking to get it to write. The soldiers had them in the First World War. So Charlie, who might have been in his sixties at that time, stood all day and every day, rain or shine, on Victoria Bridge, waving the big green buses in and out, consulting his watch, shaking his head, and very frequently licking his bit of pencil. Everyone was nice to him. All the drivers and conductors acted along, pretending he was in charge, and even the real supervisor, who had a little office on the bridge, took it in good part and you might see the pair of them, the real one and the mad one, in a slack time sharing tea from a thermos. But that day I didn't look at Charlie, though I normally did, looked and looked, I sat on the front seat, from where you had a view, if you wanted it, of Telephone House on your right, Exchange Station and the cathedral on your left, the dirty river under you, and I undid the girl's present which she had wrapped very carefully and tied up with a red ribbon. I believe I was alone on the upper deck. I believe all behind me was empty space.

It was a Wilfred Owen she had given me, and on a scrap of paper, that looked torn out of a Woolworth's notebook, she had written: Here are his poems for you. With love from M. That was when I learned her name began with 'M'. First I looked to see how long the poet had lived. I had taken to doing that. I saw that if I were him I'd be two-thirds through my allotted time already. Then I opened his book, nowhere particular, as I thought, and the space behind my back filled up with cold, it felt like a finger tracing my spine and inserting a tip of cold into the back of my head so that the hairs stood up there, I had ice around the heart and I lost the sight of his lines in a rush of tears. Then Charlie consulted his pocket watch, waved us away, licked his blue copy-pencil and made a note in his notebook of the exact time of day that particular 64 left Victoria Bridge for Peel Green.

The Irwell is the boundary between Manchester and Salford. The buses leaving Victoria Bridge cross it, back into Manchester, bear left along it past the cathedral and the station, and, turning sharp left, cross it again, back into Salford, and away. The man had been in the water for some time when I joined the others watching, and a couple of frogmen were in there with him, trying to push his head and shoulders through a life-belt, to haul him up. They had a hard task, he was so sodden and unhelpful. One took his head by the hair and tugged. The face was blue-grey. I realized that must be one of the colours of death, nothing that colour could be alive, or not in any way friendly to human beings at least.

Though I didn't know I would never see M. again – it was only a couple of days since she had given me the poems and we often went that long or longer without meeting – I was already beginning to be anxious. I had to talk to her about Wilfred Owen; and while I was watching the men in the water under Victoria Bridge I was wondering whether I should tell her about this event, and how I would say it if I decided to.

High above the river, just below street level, on a rather ramshackle platform affixed to the bridge, two policemen were watching their colleagues in the water and handling the ropes by which the drowned man was to be hauled up. I thought you might get to the platform through the supervisor's little office on the street side of the parapet. Had the river been a sweeter place he and Charlie might have taken their tea out there, on a balcony with a view. Friedrich Engels, working just round the corner in Chetham's Library on *The Condition of the Working Class in England*, thought the river and its dwelling-places supremely noxious. Poor river, it had a coal mine at the very outset and more and more demands and abuses through the cotton towns below. All its tributaries harmed it. But there were blessings nonetheless, reprieves and survivals, woods, for example, beyond the sewage farm at Clifton, and bluebells in season, hyacinthine streams and pools, like a surrogate living water. For the body of the Irwell was largely effluent, it needed what humans spilled into it to keep going at all. The rain itself came heavily laden and before it reached the river must take on the further cargo of the gutters and the drains. The Irwell was never much of a waterway, and under the bridge and the sheer side of Telephone House there was little movement. Of his own accord, so to speak, the drowned man might have idled for ever in the dead stillness under Victoria Bridge.

The policemen took off their jackets and began to haul. In shirt-sleeves on that dismal perch they looked like snowbirds. The drowned man, fitted through the life-belt, rose in the water into a semblance of buoyancy, but very soon after that, when he was tiptoe on the surface as though they were puppeteers and now they would get him to dance, the operation went wrong. The deadweight of him was too much for their arrangement of ropes. He slipped from the ring and was upended, noosed tightly around the ankles, the ring banging uselessly against his back. Water returned to the river from his jacket sleeves. We could smell it. There he hung, his clothes undoing around his midriff, hung and twirled very slowly, streaming. The frogmen assessed him. The police on the platform waited. It seemed his ropes would hold. It seemed they must risk it. At a signal, again they began to haul. Abattoir, martyrdom, circus, theatre, ascension. We were all very quiet. I decided I would tell the girl on the bus what I was seeing. I thought of the words. I felt certain she would understand what was happening to me while I watched. Suddenly there was a rush of things I must tell and ask the girl on the bus. Was her grandfather a soldier? Was his name in the book in the cathedral? And all the things my mother had begun to tell me, about the Blitz, how she and her best friends in Telephone House had volunteered to carry on working during a raid and the searchlights lit up the sky and soon they could hear the guns and the bombs. And her and my father courting: Ringley Woods, the bluebells, and how in the leap year 1936, egged on by the other girls, while the supervisor's back was turned, she phoned him at his work in the Post Office from hers on the top floor of Telephone House, and asked him to marry her. Things of that sort, so much, so many stories, all in a rush. By way of thanks for the poems of Wilfred Owen. Tell her and ask her. The drowned man twirled very slowly upside down in the lovely light of day, the water still running off him, a precious silver. And slowly he rose, with pauses, with rests in the air, hanging down, his hands come together like a diver's, everyone watching, all silent.

It was perhaps the beginnings of my father's illness that made my mother, that spring and summer, begin to tell me stories about the two of them in their early lives. He was slipping into something that neither of them understood and perhaps she wanted to assure herself of him by saying aloud how definite and luminous still their beginnings were. The remoteness of depression is hard to bear. Some acts of suicide in it may spring from the desire to be finally definite again. All the more definite around the depressive must the people who love him be, and perhaps that was an unconscious motive in my mother's stories: to make me her ally in knowing some things for sure. The cheerfulness of the girls high up in Telephone House was one such thing, how she proposed to him in the leap year with some of them watching her face for the answer in it and some further off watching out for the supervisor. And under the air raid all together, the lights and the noise, that was a brave thing to remember when it looked as though isolation by an illness might be coming up. But I liked best her assertion that on a clear day from the top floor of Telephone House she could see Ringley Woods where they went picking bluebells and came back on the bus with an armful and she slept against his shoulder in the scent of them lying in her lap like a child. And beyond Ringley, on a clear day, you could see the moors, level and high, and once up there, as is well known, you can walk out together for ever.

That spring and early summer, now I come to think of it, there must have been something about me that was asking for stories, because if it wasn't my mother telling them it was her mother and I stood or sat or strolled between the generations of women and listened to whatever they wanted to tell me about the girls at Ermen and Engels Mill or Telephone House and courtships before the first war or the second, long courtships, engagements, marriages. I watched my father anxiously, willing him with my mother not to go absent on us, and my grandfather − 'blown to bits', as his widow said whenever she reached that point, said with a shrug − him, my mother's father, I was beginning to put together again, his life till then, till the blowing to bits, collecting him up, so to speak, from her bits of story and the documents. So to speak. There is no liveliness of words comes anywhere near the life of life itself.

At the last, the drowned man's feet caught under the platform and one policeman had to kneel, leaving the other taking all the weight. It was only then I noticed that he wore decent Oxford shoes. He turned my way, his tie hung over his open mouth. They meant no indecency, I am sure, but in getting their burden over the railing of the rickety platform they could not be gentle. They reached, heaved, landed him. He lay then over the railings, arms down and between his arms his head, the hair neatly plastered forward by the foul water in a V. He wore a suit. He was perhaps in his mid-forties. I could see him with a briefcase, conscientiously going to work and back. The policeman left him there, flopped, as though after a tremendous exertion mortally exhausted. They exited through the supervisor's office and soon returned with a stretcher. Then it was finished, the spectacle. The crowd remembered their own business.

I went for my bus, a 66, got the front right seat upstairs, and craned up to see the very roof of Telephone House. There was a white cloud or two, the high building seemed to be sailing. The bus filled up, mostly young women from their work, nattering and laughing. On the bridge the ambulance had taken the drowned man away; the policemen, still in their dazzling shirtsleeves, were having a cup of tea. Things were resuming, but not fast enough for Charlie. I doubt if he had watched the spectacle at all. He was in the road itself before the queue of buses, very agitated, tapping his watch and shaking his head. Suicide's one thing, but what about the buses? What about the timetable? His trouble was manifest and helpless. My pity, quickened by one thing and another, went out to him there on the public bridge in such an anxiety. He beckoned hard, stepped aside, we pulled away. I watched him lick his pencil and make the necessary note. Mustn't forget Charlie when I tell all this to the girl on the 42.

PARIS

A Man of the Streets

JACQUES RÉDA

It was a very cold winter's night when I came across Georges Louis in front of a department store on the Left Bank, not far from the statue of Madame Boucicaut as Charity enthroned in the exercising of her office like a justification for the existence of the poor. Yet Georges Louis was not really one of the poor; more what was known in Madame Boucicaut's day as an indigent. He kept away from the little band of rather rowdy down-and-outs who at that time were permanently blockading one of the store's entrances, the one in front of the huge *de luxe* grocery department – undoubtedly a strategic spot, where customers, reluctant to put their hand in their pockets as they went in, did on occasion think to keep a coin in readiness for on the way out, or else unburden themselves of a packet of biscuits, if not a bottle of vintage wine. Some time after this, no doubt after a series of complaints, the police were to evacuate this collection of noisy, filthy drunks. But Georges Louis had already been rejected from their company because of his behaviour, which was in no way violent or aggressive. He was a solitary type, a man given to thinking a great deal and very disinclined to conform to the often barbaric rules observed by people of this milieu. So he had gone off to take up a position some tens of metres away, in the run-down area where the wall of the Laennec hospital begins. With his hands stuck into the pockets of a coat that was wearing thin and was not very clean, you might have thought he was waiting for a bus, not begging. His style was minimalist. Far from obstructing the path of passers-by and accosting them in that arrogant, amusing or contrite manner practised by most beggars, he did no more than execute a small step in his chosen direction and, without even extricating one or other of his hands, uttered his request in a scarcely audible, unconvincing voice that almost seemed to hope for a refusal. Though I walked that pavement every evening I might never have noticed his presence there, had not the unexpected arrival of a trolley loaded with old packing boxes forced him on this occasion from his usual position and thrust him straight across my path. Suddenly there we were up against one another. I saw before me a face invaded by a fortnight's growth of beard, an expression that was serene, almost smiling, eyes that were a little febrile but extremely gentle. I couldn't tell how old he was. (I later learned that he was about the same age as me.) A reflex, provoked by the possible imminence of a collision, made him raise his open palm to the level of my chest. But however swiftly he tried to stop it, his hand described, out of habit, a curve which placed it for a second horizontally, palm upward; and that is how I came to seal our relationship, by a misunderstanding that could not be prevented.

Countless times during that period of snow and ice (it was impossible for me to get him to agree to come to a café) we walked together round and round the store, from the last display – of flowers – to the statuette of the Egyptian *fellah* carrying jars. Yet Georges Louis was not very talkative. And, as I did not dare to encourage him into more confidences than he spontaneously offered, I did not learn anything especially interesting or intimate about him. Perhaps at times he felt he did not really exist; which might also have induced him to doubt the existence of other people, especially if – like mine – that existence manifested itself in the form of a sympathy lacking any objective foundation. I believe he thought of me as a sort of ghost who appeared sporadically, half-probable, and whose reappearance filled him at that time with a vague sense of surprised pleasure; after which, because of other more pressing circumstances, he forgot all about me. I was simply one element disappearing down the rue de Sèvres, between seven and eight o'clock in the evening, between the jolly fat shoplady in her widow's weeds and the athletic-looking peasant of the Nile. So Georges Louis's curiosity on my account remained reticent. But I appreciated this reserve, which was not exactly indifference, and which corresponded with my own personal feelings about precariousness and immediacy.

Georges Louis seemed both resigned to his fate, which was indeed slightly below the poverty line, and surprised, almost cheery, at the happy chance which saved him from foundering completely. It must be said he wasn't hard to please. While our relationship lasted he was congratulating himself on having discovered a rather cosy little pad in the sixteenth arrondissement; that is to say, on some newly-carpeted stairs at the top of a block of flats. By a lucky chance, or perhaps through cunning, he had found out how to slip in there at around midnight and, although he had no watch, let alone an alarm clock, he got out at ten to five on the dot next morning, just before the concierge did his rounds. Then he walked across Paris to the twelfth arrondissement where a small community of nuns gave him bread and coffee. After that he wandered round looking for some small employment, until it was time for him to take up his position again next to the Egyptian *fellah*. During that same period he enjoyed the somewhat dubious delights of having a job which lasted only three days. He managed to carry out a fairly difficult task (sticking labels on parcels) but, in the end, and in spite of the decent clothes I had given him (or at least 'lent' him, in order not to wound his natural pride) he was fired for being inappropriately dressed since it annoyed his co-workers and put off the customers. He took this new blow of fate philosophically. When we parted, he would go off in the direction of one or other of the popular soup-kitchens, and then, in a leisurely way, return to his soft, warm landing in the area of Ranelagh or Jasmin.

Owing to the fact that we were both reserved, we soon had nothing but his wanderings for our real subject of conversation. He knew the city better than anyone and could have found his way round it with his eyes closed. But as far as he was concerned it was an indifferent place, where everything was of more or less equal interest. He had slept in most of the metro stations of the capital, but had rarely used this means of transport, preferring instead to take roundabout routes through the city's labyrinth of streets, to make the journeys which separated those few connecting points in his life last longer. He thus had a very good idea of the relative situation of bridges, monuments, squares, churches, and friendly shops, which he only patronized when absolutely necessary. But my observations and questions drew forth from him nothing but an elusive or perplexed smile. I gave up asking. You might as well ask a ship's stoker to describe the delights of a cruise. I backed off. I had next to me the true man of the streets, pure and simple, a creature driven by the dictates of its stomach, while behind the silent stone and glass facades, the digestions of the hypothetical beings of whom I was a strange representative took their course.

After our very first encounters, I naturally enough soon felt out of place. I suppose that Georges Louis must have likewise felt uncomfortable. An unforeseen impulse, involuntary so to speak, had brought us together – like the eddying of a capricious wind on the streets. But the coin – scarcely asked for, scarcely given, scarcely taken – that I had held out to him was already weighing too heavily. And each new coin accentuated the false equilibrium in the subtle balance of our friendship. It disconcerted both of us that our exchanges were getting us nowhere. Louis was in fact much too modest to imagine that his company and his trust – from time to time – were enough for me. And then again he would no doubt have loved to give me something in return – but what? So it was my 'dominant economic position' which falsified our relationship. And, as we should certainly have waited in vain for him to attain my position, even if he were to stick thousands of labels on parcels, ought I not to have renounced my relative opulence, in order to get closer to him in his adversity? I was not brave enough. I did not go and sleep in the metro or on a landing in the sixteenth arrondissement, I did not try the Picpus nuns' coffee; my disappearance into the streets remained comfortably literary. At the same time, spurred on by a bad conscience, I got carried away by my generosity. For why only one coin and not several, or a bank note? Why simply old clothes and not the price of a decent hotel room? Like Madame Boucicaut, for want of knowing how to hand out a part of my fortune discreetly, I dispensed the water from my jar, like the Egyptian *fellah*, without counting the cost. I was losing my sense of proportion and becoming importunate.

A more lavish gift still must have struck terror into the heart of Georges Louis. He vanished for a week and I saw him only once after that: affable but distant, he excused himself, on the unlikely pretext of some pressing errand. Where could I go to look for him? Under what porch, in which hospital, under the roof of which block of dwellings? Remembering his anecdotes about the brutal society he moved in, I have sometimes imagined he might have been murdered. But I am not convinced. I am still expecting to come across him in the course of my ramblings, entrenched in some dark, ill-chosen corner, sheltered from the excesses of his peers and the abuses of philanthropists. If that should come about, although I miss his friendship, which was completely without any self-interest, I should attempt to make my escape before he recognized me. In fact I am persuaded that Georges Louis left me because of his finer feelings, as if he had decided he had nothing better he could offer me. To refuse this gift would be a rather unworthy act on my part. But I have another explanation, a more tortuous one: they were unwilling *on high* that I should acquire merit by disinterestedly helping my neighbour. It is not permitted to everybody to do so. That is the rule. Georges Louis's mission was perhaps to make me understand this. And that might be why I have sometimes had the feeling that he regarded me with a profound and helpless pity.

Translated from the French by Helen Constantine

REYKJAVIK

The First Day of the Fourth Week

ÁGÚST BORGÞÓR SVERRISSON

9:30

The toilet mat, a shaggy green rag which is meant to lie on the tiles next to the toilet base, curved into a semicircle which fits snugly to the base where it meets the floor. But the mat is never in its place, at best, it lies somewhere near to the toilet, at worst, in a bundle in a corner. Had he been asked a few weeks ago if there was a lavatory mat in his home, he would have been unable to answer that question. Now he recalls having seen the wife take this mat out of the washing machine and hang it up on a washing line. He might even have done it himself sometime, without giving any thought to what this was, this wet, green thing.

Why on earth does a mat like this exist? Is it better that the pee which misses the bowl lands on a green mat so it becomes saturated with piss? His wife also scrubs the tiles every weekend; does she find that it is better to have to do both that and put the mat in the washing machine?

10:00

The heating. Radiation heating doesn't bother you as long as you don't think about it. So far he has had other things to think about. But now as he finds himself at home in the middle of the day instead of coming home in the evening, his mind still on the job, now as he suddenly finds himself alone with himself in this house, the buzz of the heating pipes suddenly starts to ring very loudly in his ears, reminding him that there are no radiators in the house, that the heating is in the walls. This came as a shock to him at the time they bought the townhouse, awoke in him a brief sense of insecurity, and then came the story of the accident which had once taken place in the house on the far end of the row. He had seen for himself the large moisture stain in the kitchen there.

He has not thought about this for many years. But what if one of the pipes bursts today? Tomorrow? A month from now? Sometime when you least expect it. Hot water flows into the concrete, causing it to crumble, in a short time the conditions will be like in a damp-ridden basement. The whole house might even be destroyed.

10:30

Did the kitchen tap start to drip before he lost his job or did he just not notice it before? He turns off both the hot and the cold water taps, tight. As tight as he can. But the dripping does not let up. There is a pipe wrench down in the storage room and he should be able to fix this, but the thought of attempting it and failing is more than his self-esteem can bear these days, so he decides not to. But the dripping grows constantly louder in his ears, accompanied by the buzzing of the heating pipes; this is the music to the image of the toilet mat in his mind.

11:00

How is he supposed to dress now? The wardrobe contains a collection of inexpensive suits, single jackets and trousers, shirts and ties. These are the work clothes he has put on daily, for years, without thinking, at random, almost without seeing what his hands pulled out of the wardrobe each time. But as he does not have any reason to visit an employment agency today, no reason even to pop into a bank, has no other reason to go out than to get out of the loud silence of the house, it does not seem appropriate to dress like he normally would; it would seem like a silly denial of the situation. And yet if he puts on jeans or a tracksuit, it is like a declaration that he has become inactive.

After a long deliberation he settles on a compromise, puts on a blue suit and a light blue shirt but leaves out the tie. He is pleased with his reflection in the mirror: the blue outfit is familiar and evokes a memory of normal days, the absence of a tie an appropriate acknowledgement of the change in situation.

12:00

He has always covered his back and already in the first week he managed to sell the 4x4, something which came in handy as he is owed many months' salary. In the second week he contacted four employment agencies and applied for ten positions. In the third week he saw the employment agents again but the only news they had for him, each in their own words, was that these things took time.

Now the fourth week has begun and there is nothing to do except wait. Keep the mobile phone switched on when he is away from the house and check his email now and then.

4x4-less, he stands at the bus stop and waits there for a quarter of an hour. Finally a yellow bus arrives. Last time he travelled by bus, the buses were green. Back then they were also crammed with passengers, people on their way to and from work, students, elegant ladies. Sometimes the air on the buses was heavy with the smell of fish because of the fish factory workers, who have long since vanished from the city.

Now it is as if he steps into a less travelled parallel reality: inside the bus are three East-Asian people, and a young man having a loud conversation with himself. He is wearing a torn denim jacket and his dirty hair sticks up into the air.

One more passenger joins the bus on the way: a very short man who trundles ahead of him three black plastic bags, packed with refundable containers. The bags stack up as high as the man's head and for the remainder of the journey he struggles to stay on his feet and to stop the bags from drifting around the bus. It is strange and almost fascinating to watch such a primitive fight for survival. The man does not look very elderly, for his body is too quick and firm. But his face is still covered in deep wrinkles. His skin is brown from dirt, not dark, but light brown, yet you can tell that this is not a suntan.

The smell coming off him is foreign and ambiguous, does not evoke repulsion, but rather a vague curiosity.

12:45

He has never been much of a café man, but has occasionally gone to one near to his workplace on his lunch break when he has become bored with the cafeteria. Now he cannot think of any other place to go as he finds himself in the city centre for no reason. He feels like he is on a lunch break at work as he steps inside, but that feeling goes away quickly. Sitting at one table are civil servants whose faces he recognises, a woman and three men. The woman nods towards him. She has not greeted him before, he is stunned and reacts too slowly to return her greeting, and by then she has turned away, absorbed in conversation.

He orders the same as usual, a coffee and a bread roll with cheese. But he has no appetite now. He has not eaten anything today, does not want to admit to himself that he has lost all appetite, and silently curses himself for having ordered this, since he is not hungry and now the roll sits untouched on the plate like a symbol of some misery.

Four young builders in blue overalls are sitting at one of the tables, eating soup out of small bowls and nibbling at mini-slices of French baguette. This meal is as ill-suited to them as ballet dancing, those big and burly men of hard labour. But it is probably a sign of the times, the most unlikely people have begun to follow health tips, gulping down water all day long and eating light meals. And food has for some reason become much more fattening than it was a few decades ago. Back then men like this would have eaten a heavy lunch of meat, but would still have been thinner than these blokes.

After a while people go back to their jobs and the place empties, apart from a blind man who sits in a corner and talks to himself. This is the second man he encounters today who talks to himself. He wonders if there will be more before the day's out.

A good while later a chubby young man enters the café. His head is downcast, he is quite front-heavy and his movements are a bit sluggish, but a smile plays on his lips.

'I would like a large Danish pastry and cocoa with whipped cream, please,' he says to the waitress in a voice which could only be described as a loud whisper. 'It is my birthday today, you see,' he adds shyly when the food is on the table. The waitress does not respond to this but looks uneasy. This does not faze him and he says: 'I am 29 years old today,' and laughs. He then begins to talk to himself in that loud whisper and it is just as if he and the blind man in the corner are having a conversation.

He has another cup of coffee himself and continues to sit there, far too long. He reads the papers. One of them contains a news article on the liquidation, speculation that some money has been stashed away. He reads a few obituaries. He can not remember having done that before. They are extremely dull. He reads 'Readers' Letters'. A woman writes that she has seen men's shoes at a good price in Europris. A coat has been taken by mistake from a pub in Grafarvogur. An old man complains about communion wine he had drunk a year ago, that it tasted bitter. He hopes that this has been remedied.

He has a third cup of coffee. His stomach lets out loud gurgling sounds, not unlike the sound of a coffeemaker. The roll sits untouched on the white plate. He wonders how long it will take before it gets hard. It seems to him that the cheese slice has already begun to darken.

15:00

Why is he surprised? He knew better than this. What did he expect? Nonetheless it is a shock to him to see the empty and deserted company buildings. There is no sign of life here. For the last months they only worked on one floor in the old factory, and the cafeteria was still on the top floor of the newspaper building. Everything else was standing empty by then, but he paid no attention to it. There he sat every day, and believed the repeated promises which now sound ridiculous.

The newspaper building has in fact stood empty for a whole year, ever since the paper was sold; the other companies went into liquidation. In this building he started his career more than 20 years ago and he once had a small office there on the top floor. Recently his advancement had been very rapid. As the other managers of the conglomerate fled in droves, he was constantly being promoted, to the point when he was second in charge to the owner, a man who had barely greeted him previously but was no longer the big entrepreneur he was before, because everything had shrunk.

In two buildings further south had been a small magazine publishing company, a radio station and a telemarketing business. All gone and the buildings empty.

In the old factory building was the other newspaper, the offices of its online counterpart, and an advertising agency. When the conglomerate began its operation in this building, there was talk that the factory belonged to an industry of the past and that now the future was moving into the building. The new factory, by contrast, is thriving; located at Grandi in the western part of the city, they do night shifts there and the machines are churning away 24 hours a day. Next to the old factory building was the print shop. It shut down two months ago.

The silence of the grave settles over him here. He has rarely felt such shame. He knows this is not his fault, but he was a part of it, believed the promises, stupidly worked at the same company for almost a quarter of a century and is now standing in the street, staring at the blank windows of buildings emptied of people.

Above all this seems unreal to him. Like in a stupid nightmare, the fact that he cannot enter the old factory building now, sit down at his desk and continue to work. Is it not actually more likely that he is sitting there now and is imagining this nonsense? That the person standing out here is a figment of the mind, his own imagination?

16:00

After a long, aimless but rather refreshing walk he goes into the bus station building. On light-brown lacquered wooden benches sit people who seem to be waiting for their luck to turn. Yet judging from their facial expressions, they have given up all hope but are still stubbornly waiting. Indistinct ages, coarse facial features, dirty hair and dirty clothes. The overall appearance shows the tell-tale signs of substance abuse, yet no one appears drunk or in an altered state at the moment.

He thinks to himself that at this time of day all the normal people are at work, but the weirdos hang out in cafés and bus station buildings and ride on the half-empty buses. Now he is with the weirdos.

He looks at his watch and it surprises and frightens him how time has flown. He has always been able to get a lot done quickly, and it is amazing to think how fast one can get used to doing nothing – time passes all the same.

For years he has moved through this area to go to the bank, or to a shop, or to fetch the car from a car park down here on the west side when he could not find a spot up on the hill. Yet all this time he has never set foot in the bus station. And now when he finally comes in here, it is for no particular purpose, he who has never gone anywhere without a reason, never done anything without a purpose; although it now all seems to have been purposeless, all his toil throughout the years.

He decides to invent an errand by going to the gents', squeeze out a few drops and wash his hands.

He is shocked by his reflection in the mirror. In his expression he detects the shame he experienced earlier in the deserted work area, and the same hopelessness he detected in the expressions of the people on the wooden benches out in the waiting hall. His face seems dirty, the suit wrinkled and covered in stains, and there is also a spot on the shirt. It may be because of the peculiar light in here, how the lighting is reflected off the yellow walls. He did not look this bad in the mirror at home. For a moment it occurs to him that one always looks the way one feels.

17:45

They have not had a row since he lost his job. The memory of the constant arguments makes him nostalgic, it is a memory of security. Mainly they were about him being too absent-minded, and her having to be responsible for everything. He usually responded by listing the chores that he did. She said he did not do them properly and she had to organize all the work. He then said that he worked more than her and earned a higher salary. She said he was rarely at home and when he was at home his mind was always somewhere else.

Now there is not a cross word from her. No criticisms, nothing. She does not even ask him how the job search is going. She is silent and friendly. He fears that she will explode one day and there will be an almighty row.

Now the sink is filled with dirty dishes and the dishwasher is filled with clean ones. She asked him to do the kitchen this morning. Still sitting in the hall is the bag he was supposed to take down to the laundry room and empty into the machine. He forgot all this and now she has begun to prepare the meal in the dirty kitchen, having just arrived home from work, he has not lifted a finger all day. Never before has he been such an easy target, never has his cause been as hopeless, and therefore he feels as if a row has already started, although she does not say a word.

Despairing, he rushes to the bathroom and calls her from there. She emerges in the doorway, her face one big question mark.

'You, who's so perfect, why do you have this ridiculous mat here in the bathroom?' His voice shakes, he jerks his hand back and forth over the tiles and begins to ramble: '... piss mat... unhygienic... make-work... pointless...'

She answers calmly that it is only there for decorative purposes and points to an identically-coloured mat in the centre of the floor below the sink. He stares at this mat for a long time, has never noticed it before, but realises that it has been there for many years. And now, unusually, the toilet mat is level and straight, in its proper place. He looks from one mat to the other and now sees in them nothing but perfect harmony.

Defeated, he meets her glance but reads no victory in her eyes, she is just worried. Softly she says that dinner will be ready soon.

23:30

In bed, the day flashes through his head in disparate fragments: a yellow bus, black plastic bags, deep wrinkles, a bread roll on a white plate, blank windows in the old factory building, a blue suit, a fat man eating a Danish pastry, bad communion wine, small soup bowls, blue overalls, the dripping from the kitchen tap, the woman from the ministry's nod, cheap men's shoes, a blind man talking to himself. The day is a collection of pointless and sad details and he feels there is no unity in the world anymore.

But then he tries to think about the mats in the bathroom again, a green mat by the toilet base, a green mat beneath the sink, and he senses the harmony, a perfect green harmony and the green colour spreads across his mind's eye, turning into a meadow stretching out further than the eye can see.

He can feel her hand on his. He hesitates, then he squeezes her hand and she squeezes his in return. As he drifts off into sleep he feels her speaking to him in a soothing voice, reassuring words, but it is only a dream; she is inside her own dream, tossing and turning in the dark.

Translated from the Icelandic by Vera Juliusdottir

BARCELONA

The Inferior Quality of Contemporary Poetry

EMPAR MOLINER

In order to write *Provincial Lover*, Eladi Susaeta has had to ask for a six-month leave of absence from the private university at which he teaches the Masters degree in journalism. He's never done anything like this before. It's never taken him longer than two or three weeks to finish a book. He writes, in fact, in an almost automatic way. He finished *The Emperor Goes Naked*, a critique on the mediocrity of contemporary literature, in twenty days. *Against Nationalism and Other 'Isms'* was harder work, it's true, but that's only because it took on the form of an engagements diary. And *The Burner Alchemist*, the gastronomic journey through the life of chef Carlo Puig, he actually wrote over an Easter Bank Holiday weekend. But *Provincial Lover* is something altogether different. It's the most important challenge Susaeta's ever had to face. 'We see in you a spokesman of progress, modern, we see you as representing the new Barcelona, the liberated Barcelona, the one that faces the future, not the past,' the town hall's commissioner told him. 'We want you to apply your *The Emperor Goes Naked* theories to this job.' And he couldn't say no.

Provincial Lover will be the lyrics to the song they'll use in the advert to promote Barcelona during the Worldwide State Leader's Meeting. The flamenco singer El Chaco will perform it, and the text is to be printed over a sketch by the painter Garolera. The advert will be broadcast on TV and printed in newspapers all over Europe, the United States and Japan. Susaeta has estimated more people will read his work like this in one single day, than otherwise in his whole lifetime. With this in mind, during the whole of his leave of absence he hasn't once gone wine tasting in the local wineries, nor has he engaged with new controversies on the radio, nor tried to seduce any of his Masters students. His life is now devoted to *Provincial Lover*.

He serves himself a whisky, closes his office door so the cleaning lady can't hear and recites out loud the latest result of his efforts:

Provincial Lover

I leave my words
—discreet—here.
The little money I have
and the books, next to
the whisky glass.

And, above all, the flamenco.

I leave the immigrant girl's CDs,
she's hot,
and doesn't care about nationalisms.
I'm a *xarnego*[*] jumping off the ship, but you girl, no,
don't leave.
Not you, don't leave, Barcelona.

---

[*]xarnego: A pejorative Catalan term for a Spanish person, usually one who resides in Catalunya, yet doesn't use Catalan as their language of choice.

With all due modesty, he considers this excellent work. He pops the page into his manuscript file and copies it onto his computer's hard drive. He then prints out four copies. One for his ex-wife, one for his agent—also lover—, one for the journalist Ángel Gafarró, and another for Maribel, the divorcee on his Masters course whom, if all goes well, he'll be free to seduce after the campaign's official presentation.

He phones his ex-wife first of all. He lets her know he's finished the lyrics, and that he'd like to hear her opinion before submitting it to the town hall's press office. He decides to do this because, even though she tends to read Susaeta's books with superiority and disdain, he still believes she is, in her own way, a fair enough critic. For instance, when she read the proof sheets of *Against Nationalism and Other 'Isms'*, she spotted a mistake: it wasn't Eisenhower who said 'a single death is a tragedy; a million deaths is a statistic', but Churchill. But his ex-wife apologizes: she's so much on at work, these days, and simply hasn't the time for lunch.

—Read it over the phone. It can't be that long, can it?

—I don't think it's something I can read over the phone, Agnès.—Susaeta's offended she doesn't want to hold the text in her own hands.

—Well, come to the bookshop this evening and bring it with you.

He finds this even more offensive, to have to go to his ex-wife's bookshop, but he agrees to do so.

He then phones Maribel, and tells her the same: that he's finished it now. It turns out she can't do lunch, either. She can't leave work until four, so they decide he'll have lunch on his own at El Alambique, chef Carlo Puig's restaurant, and she'll turn up for coffee.

She arrives just as Susaeta's finishing off his rectangular bowl of dessert:

—I'm so excited...—she sighs, her eyes shining.—This is your first original draft, and I'm going to read it. Who else

35

has seen it?

—I wanted you to be the first. I'll only show it to my ex-wife if you approve this draft. And later today I'm meeting my agent, and a journalist who is also a sworn enemy of mine.— Seeing she laughs, he adds: —We're intimate enemies.

Maribel sucks her thumb, flirtatiously:

—But I'll not be able to make as interesting remarks as your agent. Nor am I as severe as your ex-wife. And I'm such a slow reader... I'm bound to let you down.

Susaeta wants to hear Maribel's opinion mainly to take it to bed with him. It's also true that, of all three, she's his most ardent admirer. Anna-Maria, his agent, has a cold and professional attitude, and can also be a know-all, which can be quite irritating at times.

—All I want is for you to tell me: 'the rhythm is good', or 'the rhythm doesn't work'. For you to say, 'it's good', or 'it isn't good'. It's a song which could be a poem and which can be read on many different levels, you'll find. Let's be clear about this, I don't deny it could turn out to be unsuccessful; it is subversive to a certain extent, it grew into something larger than a mere commission. It isn't obliging to those in power (if they wanted a complacent text, they came to the wrong man), nor is it the classic 'visit Barcelona'. It's the *xarnego* vision, immigration's grandchild. Reading it will make you feel, to a certain extent, uncomfortable.

Shaking, Maribel puts her glasses on and picks up the sheet of paper. Meanwhile, Susaeta orders a whisky and a cigar. He watches her read, slowly, reverential.

—Eladi...—she sighs, after she's finished reading—. Look!—She shows him her arm, so he can see it's now covered in goose bumps.

—Do you like it?

—Yes, yes, a lot. But now, I'll play devil's advocate, OK? These are just silly issues of mine.

He smiles, to encourage her to speak, but he's angry to think that, if they're no more than 'silly issues of hers', she still considers them worth bringing to his attention.

—First of all: the last sentence. I'd leave it out. You don't need it. The song is perfectly comprehensible without that line. It would make the overall message much more convincing.

Susaeta realizes she may be right. Yes, the last line is repetitive. Maybe she's right, maybe she's right that it doesn't add anything. To write is to know how to stop in time, not to want to explain everything. A poem is masculine like an orgasm. The last line must be the climax.

—And also, and maybe this is a paranoia of mine, there's the whisky.

—What's wrong with the whisky?—Maribel can be so boring sometimes.

—How can I explain?

He's exasperated. He's allowed her to read the poem to make her happy. Not because he'd wanted a doctoral thesis on it.

—Well, whisky seems almost too easy. As if it had been the first thing to enter your mind. Which, obviously, it wasn't. But, as you know, I read everything searching for double meanings, for reasons, for sense... So maybe I'm finding the whisky very... I don't know. What everyone would have written. I'm not explaining myself very well, am I?

—It isn't pondered, there is no reason. I drink whisky. I'm drinking whisky now. —He chooses one cigar of the many the waiter is offering him.

—Yes, of course, take no notice. It's like the flamenco thing. It seems clichéd to mention flamenco, as if that were the first thing to enter your mind as well. Yet at the same time, I realize both issues have more to do with my perfectionism than with your writing.

He agrees, eager to change the course of their

conversation. This is what happens when you accept divorcees onto Masters courses. Their opinions are miles away from the opinions he teaches his students to have. He spends his days, after all, telling them every word they write is clichéd and dull. Warning them not to imitate the terribly funny, banal journalists who make like monkeys on TV programmes. Telling them they must find their own voice. And now, she, to make herself sound interesting, talks about clichés. But anyway...

—Maybe I could change the whisky for, who knows, a calvados. —He says this to humour her. Deep down it's all the same to him, one drink or the other.

—Yes! Of course! Brilliant!

Seeing how sure she seems of this, he crosses out 'whisky' and writes 'calvados'. He then reads it out loud:

I leave my words
—discreet— here.
The little money I have
and the books, next to
the calvados glass.

—That's perfect!—she exclaims.—Can you see the difference?

—It worked better with two syllables. I could change it to 'cognac'.

—Eladi...— she pauses. —Cognac, of course, it has to be cognac.

—Cognac. Maybe you're right.

—And it's the same with 'flamenco'. Flamenco's so clichéd, so typical... I'd prefer a lesser-known musical style, I really would. But never mind. I'm just very obsessive when it comes to clichés.

—Yes, I know, you told me.

—And the title. I'd leave the piece untitled. You don't

have to explain what it means, as if it were a work of abstract art.

He closes his eyes, as if meditating on it. It doesn't seem such a bad idea.

—Maybe you're right, I'm not saying no to any of this. Maybe I will get rid of the title.

—I love you! You're a genius! You've such great talent!—She takes off her glasses and tilts her head, as if surprised at how brave she's being. She dries the beginning of a tear with her thumb pad, and, while doing this, begins to speak without even realizing she's opened her mouth:

—And what about the ending, Eladi? You'll have to have another think about the ending. I swear you could get rid of the last line.

He admits she's right, almost convinced himself. To see it more clearly, he crosses out the line and reads:

I leave the immigrant girl's CDs,
she's hot,
and doesn't care about nationalisms.
I'm a *xarnego* jumping off the ship, but you girl, no,
don't leave.

—Can you see, Eladi? It's a thousand times more convincing like this.

He caresses her cheek and reminds her he'll have to show his ex-wife the song. Maribel finds this reasonable, but even so it irritates her. Five days ago her period ended and this would have been the perfect time to have sex with Susaeta, without having to use a condom. She's not slept with anyone since the divorce, and believes he, sensitive as he is, will not be the kind of man who pays attention to whether a woman has flabby arms or drooping breasts; that instead he'll consider a good sense of humour and complicity important. His ex-wife makes her jealous.

—The flamenco thing, think it over, OK?

He asks the waiter for the bill by pretending to make a note with his right hand. The waiter gestures with his palms, as if barring Susaeta's way, meaning that it's on the house. And Susaeta lifts his arms to the sky as if to indicate he's offended. Maribel pays close attention to the scene, to its ritual nature, with exaggerated surprise, until the porter brings their coats and helps them on with them. Once in the street, they say goodbye. Susaeta kisses her hand, thanks her and they walk off in opposite directions. She heads off towards the underground station, he takes a taxi. On the way, he notes down all the changes coherently.

When he reaches the bookshop, he finds his ex-wife and her colleague barefoot in the shop window hanging up globes and moons made from papier mâché. Straight away, she leaves what she'd been doing, puts her shoes on and asks to see the sheet of paper.

—But I'll read it in the office, you'll make me nervous if you stand there watching me—she warns him.—I'll call you when I'm ready.

To kill time, Susaeta wanders along the shelves and has a look through the books. *Stop the World, I'm Getting Off*, Marga Bel's collected journalism is no longer on the 'brand new' table, even though it was launched only ten days ago. Serves her right, thinks Susaeta. She's frivolous and always writes the same thing: of what she gets up to in the gym with her gay friends. His Masters students know this already: he can't stand her. But in the shop window and on the best-selling table there is another collection of articles: *Don't Shoot the Journalist*, by Martí Campos, some kid who took his course last year, and whom he's hated ever since. He'd thought he was the next big thing, just because he wrote about hip-hop and petrol stations. He considered himself a disciple of the journalist Àngel Garrafó, rather than his. Susaeta failed him. He didn't deserve to get a pass. Now he writes a regular column in a newspaper. Even Anna-Maria considers the things he writes to be 'cool'.

Very discreetly, Susaeta takes copies of the Fémina prizewinner, the novel *Terse Thighs*, and conceals the mountain of Campos books. His ex-wife calls him.

—Eladi!

Entering the office, the first thing he sees on the desk is his page full of scrawls, rubbed out bits, question marks, and exclamation marks, written in red. His first impression is that this is some kind of violation.

—Can we talk now, Eladi?

—Sure we can.—He finds her tone, the suggestion of mystery, irritating. She should just tell him what she thinks, without pretending she's so important.

—Shall we go for a drink?

—Can't we just deal with this now? I'm meeting Anna-Maria later, you see, and can't cancel.—He hasn't told her Anna-Maria's his lover; he knows she'd be very jealous.

—Whatever.—Susaeta can tell she's offended.

—I was the one who wanted to eat lunch with you, let me remind you.

—Sure, OK.

—Shall we have a special dinner together tomorrow?—he suggests, trying to redeem things.—Shall I reserve a table at El Alambique?

—We'll see. The sheet of paper could get stained, couldn't it?

—Sure, sure—he replies, trying to appear indifferent.—It's just a draft.

His ex-wife tells him, in principle, she likes the song, but she'd get rid of the last line. It's just not necessary to include it. To be perfectly honest, it makes sense without it, it's much more complete. Of course it doesn't do any harm either. But, what does it add? Isn't it just a bit exaggerated? If he got rid of it, wouldn't the whole thing become more serious? All this and she hasn't even got to the word 'CD', a cheap modern concession. You begin with 'CD' and end up with 'hip-hop', like Martí Campos.

Susaeta considers this, and it all seems reasonable. He already knows she'll go on to explain how she doesn't like the hotheaded way in which he speaks of the 'hot' girl. She always has to find fault in the women who appear in his books.

—Maybe like this.—He takes a pen from his breast pocket and changes a few things. He reads the final draft out loud, to test how it sounds:

I leave the immigrant girl's VINYLS,
she's hot,
and doesn't care about nationalisms.
I'm a *xarnego* jumping off the ship, but you, girl, no.

It is true it's much less obvious now, Susaeta admits. One can still see the poet is asking Barcelona not to go away. He may change it.

—I may change it.

—Do what you want, of course. It just seems so obvious to me.—She takes a deep breath:—The other thing I didn't like was the hot girl.

—But it's the soul of the poem. I can't take that out.

—I'm telling you, it's up to you. But me, *I* can't help but be shocked at how 'immigrant girl' is followed by 'she's hot'. —This almost convinces him.

He says goodbye to his ex-wife and takes another taxi. As he makes his way to Anna-Maria's literary agency, a loft in the suburb of Born, he re-writes the poem. He re-reads it as he rings the bell, and takes the stairs.

Since he's been on leave they haven't met once, but, just before then, they'd reached the point at which they'd both begun to be bored with their relationship. To go out for lunch, or to go to bed together had lost its initial thrill of novelty. They did both still, but less frequently and without much enthusiasm. He found he was more upset to perceive her boredom than his own. Physically, Anna-Maria looks like all the literary agents he knows: she's slim, short, and small breasted. She also dresses like the rest: in a beige-coloured suit.

—Is that it?—she asks, curious.

And they hug. He tells her it is.

—Who else has seen it?

—Agnès. But I'm showing it to Àngel Gafarró, too.

He doesn't say a word about his Masters student, knowing she'll suspect straight away he's trying to seduce her.

—Oh, that's good. He's a good critic, Gafa. Better than I am. I probably won't be able to tell you anything terribly interesting. Besides, as you know, it's in my nature to play devil's advocate.

While she reads, Susaeta studies the photos of the writers hung on the wall. Some are new, hadn't been there before. She represents more and more authors, Anna-Maria, and they're ever more commercial. And if each time she represents more authors, and if the authors she represents are more and more commercial, it seems unlikely she'll soon still be able to represent better quality authors well. One day they must discuss the issue seriously.

—Eladi...— Anna-Maria whispers, once she's done.

—What do you think?

—It's the best thing you've ever written.

—Would you say it's powerful?— he asks modestly.

—Very. It would be even more so if you got rid of the last line. Didn't your ex-wife think so?

—She said the same thing of a last line I already got rid of.

—Oh, right. Now I understand. That's why this ending seems incomplete now. The 'no' is an anticlimactic ending.

Whereas 'she doesn't care about nationalisms' would make it rise, go out with a bang.—To emphasize what she's saying, she presses her lips together and moves her forearm into her closed fist, as if to represent a firework going off. He takes his pen from his pocket.

I leave the hot girl's VINYLS,
she doesn't care about nationalisms.

—What do you think? she asks, satisfied.
—It does have more of an impact like this.
—It's so much more 'bang!'—and she repeats her previous gesture. To compensate, I'd write 'cognac' in capitals. You could write in capitals what you consider most important: what you drink, and the hot girl's vinyls.
—Do you like the fact I don't mention who she is?
—I think it's the best, the most intelligent thing about this song.
—Does it seem strange, that it lacks a title?
—It makes it all the more simple—she lies, since she hadn't even noticed the title was missing.
—Does 'cognac' work?
—It doesn't bother me. I'm more concerned about 'my words'.
—What do you mean?
—'I leave my words' almost sounds like a will. It's the typical thing a journalist would say. I think it's plenty to leave the money and the books. You can't really leave your words anyway, everything you ever wrote is in the library.
—But, how would you put it?
—You leave the money and the books. Full stop. It seems so much more modest like that. Much more personal, of *yourself.*
—And yet it doesn't sound right, to say: 'I leave the little money I have and the discreet books.'

—What if you wrote 'notebook'? It sounds much more humble, and, consequently, much grander somehow.

—Also, 'notebooks' are more 'discreet' than words.

—But, to be honest, Eladi, what does 'discreet' add? What does it add?

I leave the little money I have, here,
and my notebook by
the glass of COGNAC.

And, above all, the flamenco.

I leave the hot girl's VINYLS,
she doesn't care about nationalism.

Having heard it out loud, Susaeta sees it very clearly. It sounds good like this. It now sounds so minimalist. She's right. He thanks her and writes the poem out one more time. If she doesn't mind, he says afterwards, he'll leave straight away to see Àngel Gafarró. Until they publish the poster and record the advert, he's not going to be able to think about anything else; but when this is all over and done they must have dinner at El Alambique, like they used to. She consents, smiling. Deep down, she's happy he's leaving. Having not seen him for over half a year, it bores her to be with him. Besides, there's a radio presenter who's just signed a representation contract that she likes.

Susaeta meets Gafarró in the bar of a city centre hotel. The connection between them has been a strained one since the day Susaeta spoke badly of Gafarró in *Against Nationalism and Other 'Isms'*. As an act of revenge, Gafarró wrote an article mocking *The Burner Alchemist*, in which he wondered whether the owner of the chain of supermarkets which had paid for the book knew it's impossible to come across a 'sensual prawn' in *a banda* rice—not because the sensuality of prawns is yet to be proven, but quite simply because there are no prawns in *a banda* rice. For months after that, Susaeta received phone calls every night; someone asking whether that was a fishmongers', and whether they sold sensual prawns. He had to install an answering machine. Of course Susaeta could not show him the text: that way he'd expose himself to fierce criticism in *Ambigú*, the magazine for which Gafarró writes under a pseudonym.

Upon meeting, Gafarró announces almost straight away he's hard up and would love a toasted ham and cheese sandwich. Susaeta knows he does this on purpose, in order to force him to have to remind him in a hotel such as this they don't serve ham and cheese sandwiches.

—Oh, Susaeta, if only I knew the important people you know, and got commissions to write easy stuff like you do...—Gafarró sighs, while patting him on the back. He always pretends to be broke in front of Susaeta.

He starts to read, and almost immediately points out you don't drink cognac from a glass, but that maybe his fans won't mind this, being used, after all to incongruities in his books. He also mentions it's cynical to write about the 'little money' next to the wrong glass, when taking into account the amount he's been paid to write this song. It would be more honest not to specify how much money there is. On the other hand, it doesn't seem logical to leave just one notebook, since he's bound to own many. Nor does it make any sense that a line such as 'She doesn't care about nationalisms' should be the one to end the poem with. He should have known to end the whole thing in time. It would have been far far better to end with the hot girl and her vinyls.

That night, Susaeta locks himself in his office and re-writes:

I leave the money I have, here,
by the drink of COGNAC.

And above all, the flamenco.

I leave the hot girl's VINYLS.

The following day, he hands in the result to the painter
Garolera, for him to illustrate. Garolera reckons the song is
sublime, or would be without the last line that, according to
him, is superfluous.
—Playing devil's advocate, I'll let you know I can't see
the point of some anonymous girl ending the song. It's as if
the text works on two levels. One, very intimate—the first
part— and the other, too vague. 'Girl' and 'hot' just don't
follow on from 'next to the drink of cognac.'
Susaeta realizes his point couldn't be more true. He goes
home, has dinner in a hurry, locks himself in his study, rubs
out the last line, and looks at the result.

I leave the money I have, here
by the drink of COGNAC.

And above all, the flamenco.

It's perfect. To re-write, to re-write is the secret of any
creator. He's already decided: his next book will be a critique
of the inferior quality of all contemporary poetry being
composed in this country today. He's already decided on the
book's first line: 'Whoever said 'your teeth are pearls' the very
first time, was a genius. Whoever said it last, is an idiot.'
The following day he eats at El Alambique with the
town hall's press manager, the one who commissioned the
song. After dessert, he reads the text and congratulates him:
it's a masterpiece of the essential. So much so he believes—

and it's only the modest opinion of a profane man—it isn't necessary to say: 'the money I have'. He doesn't think it's necessary to point out it's the author's money. It is enough to mention 'the money'. Above all, because the song is directed to people the world over, the idea they must get is that this is not a closed country of mean people, preoccupied by matters of economy. Quite the opposite. It's necessary to tell of a generous, open, Mediterranean people. As for the cognac, everyone should drink what they like best, of course, but it's such a shame the 'I' narrator—since he does drink—doesn't drink Catalan wine, cava, or, at least, a liquor more local to the country described.

—'Wine' kills the line's rhythm—Susaeta defends himself—and I can't write 'glass of cava' when the poem is in fact a critique of provincial small town mentality!

Straight away, the press manager reassures him he understands, that he doesn't intend to limit his freedom in any way. But he insists it isn't necessary to mention flamenco in the last line. The important thing is for the whole song to sound like a will. And the will, in the writer's mind, is the money and the drink. There's too much of the 'sensitive soul' in there, once the flamenco's brought into it. And not because flamenco isn't typical Catalan music, but because it's obvious the writer will leave flamenco behind. Besides, in Garolera's sketching it will be explained, in the universal language that painting is, what Susaeta feels for flamenco. It will be perfectly comprehensible.

They try it out:

I leave the money here,
next to the drink of COGNAC.

Of course. That's what the song was meant to be. With very few words, Susaeta has managed to express the contradictory love he feels for his city; a sincere, yet critical love. He considers the poem finished now, and that same afternoon, four messengers leave the town hall with copies for the composer, the editor, the advert's director and the singer.

Two days later, Susaeta goes over the proofs. He almost has a heart attack when he finds they've, by error, written 'cognac' in the lower case. The person responsible tells him it's now impossible to correct anything, because they'd trusted Susaeta wouldn't want to make any changes, and the text has been at the printers for hours.

—They're a gang of civil servants—he complains to Anna-Maria, while she, on her knees, her head level with his flies, tries to console him.

Maribel phones him, moved, having received a copy of the poster and the CD. The song is beautiful, and she's so happy he listened to the advice she had to offer. Above all, she's happy he decided to leave 'cognac' in the lower case. She'd thought it best when she saw the last draft, but hadn't dared bring up the issue. His ex-wife makes no comment.

All through the week, there are reviews printed in all the main newspapers' culture supplements. In one, they call the poem a 'masterpiece'; in another, the poem's referred to as 'an urban haiku composed by an outsider'. One newspaper didn't include a review, only a letter to the director branding the song a 'swindle sponsored by taxpayers'. A comedian calls it 'affected' on his radio programme, and the presenter of the only programme about books on TV (who also writes for a newspaper yet didn't bother writing a review) refers to it as 'a sick joke'. Àngel Gafarró, in *Ambigú*, praises Garolera's painting, but laments the fact Susaeta's poem, written in quite bold characters, partially covers it.

For the campaign's launch, Susaeta makes sure neither his ex-wife nor Anna-Maria receive invites. He knows Gafarró won't be there, since that same day he has to be at the Journalism College, to protest against the sacking of the editor of a radio programme.

The evening of the party, Maribel turns up in a long, silver dress, with a matching handbag in her hand, so small, that, from a distance, Susaeta had thought it was a sandwich wrapped in tinfoil. She's so eccentric, Maribel. Afterwards, relieved, he realizes his eyesight had deceived him.

—*Tu sei cosi bella...*—he compliments her. And kisses her finger tips.

The act begins. Following the mayor's speech, Garolera, the composer and the advert's director say a few words. After, it's his turn:

—If you don't mind, as usual, I'll let my work speak for me.—After which, he recites:

I leave the money here,
next to the drink of cognac.

The public applauds furiously. After which, the French translator, the next on the scene, expresses gratitude for the subsidy she has been awarded to complete the work, and explains the many difficulties she has encountered transforming Susaeta's peculiar musicality into Molière's tongue; without it losing any of its original strength. Especially when working with such tight deadlines, she adds. She puts her glasses on and reads:

Je laisse l'argent ici,
à côté de la coupe de cognac.

The translators into Italian, Galician, English, Basque and the two Japanese translators also read their versions of the poem. Someone turns the lights off and upon the cinema screen they project the advert. It shows images of the Pedrera, Sagrada Familia, and an aerial view of the city. El Chaco appears, barefoot, on the sweeping staircase of the Park Güell. The guitarist plays two chords, and El Chaco

begins: 'I leave the money here, next to the drink…' He ends
with the lament: '…of cognac.'

More clapping, one or two 'bravos'. Someone turns the
lights back on and the waiters begin serving drinks.

—Will you do me a favour?—Maribel asks Susaeta at
one point—. Would you give me the original text as a
present, and sign it for me?—And her eyes moisten.

He caresses her arm:

—It's at home. If you want, we can go back together to
drink one last whisky, and I'll give it you.

She says fine, while drying her tears. It's now fifteen days
since she had her last period, so she'll have to use a condom,
but supposes he'll have some at home. They pretend to slip
away—in fact, no one notices they're gone—and take a taxi.
On the way, they kiss, but not too much, as she acts quite coy.
Once at his flat, she needs the toilet. Susaeta makes the most
of the occasion, and writes out the poem on a cream coloured
piece of paper. When she's done in the bathroom, he hands it
to her.

—What about the date?

Susaeta adds the date.

—I'll frame it.—And so as to not leave it behind, with
all the care in the world she places it on the hall table.

They kiss on the sofa. Maribel lets Susaeta's hair down—
it had been tied up in a pony-tail—and her hands are then so
sticky with hair gel she has to wipe them on the cushion,
discreetly. He has no condoms at home, so she performs oral
sex on him (Susaeta reckons it's not as good as Anna-Maria's,
but better than Agnès') and he does the same for her, but
Maribel can't compare his performance to anyone else's, since
this is the first time anyone went down on her.

They then hug, and talk about the French version of the
song, which, maybe because the translator wasn't all that
fantastic, maybe because she was over-confident, lacks the
strength of the original. She should have got in touch with

him if she had so many doubts. They also complain about his colleagues' resentment. Nowhere else in the world, they hypothesize, do writers hate one another in such a way, when they ought to be united. But it's time for the gossip programme on Channel Three to begin, so they stop talking and watch it together. Watching this programme, rather than the sex, is what officially marks the beginning of their new relationship as a couple. They go to bed, and sleep in a 44 shape.

The next day, she gets up at seven, because she prefers to shower at home and get changed before going to work. They agree to have lunch at El Alambique together. Susaeta then idles until eight, and at nine goes to the newspaper library to get some initial research done for his book on the inferior quality of contemporary poetry (he wants it ready and done in two weeks). What with one thing and another, he doesn't notice that Maribel forgot to pick up the poem.

The person who does notice it is the cleaning lady, when she comes to clean the flat at eleven. She puts her glasses on, and reads. She looks, intrigued, on the table. She just doesn't get Susaeta. Can't see the drink of cognac anywhere. So, where on earth has he left the money?

Translated from the Catalan by Laura Pros Carey

From Superwoobinda

ALDO NOVE

The Carnage on Via Palestro

When I went to the carnage on Via Palestro with my girlfriend, Capricorn, she was dressed like a tart.

This could look disrespectful, especially since she had on black, tight trousers, but no-one seemed to notice, because when you're in front of carnage you don't even notice pussy.

At first, that evening everything's normal, then say your husband, or your wife, goes to Via Palestro and ends up as small chunks on the trees and ground and on the bonnets of cars parked two hundred metres away, and they can't find, say, a bit of their back, and that's your husband in the bodybags.

Everybody thinks about the dead.
Me too. I'm twenty. Walking through the crowds, I saw the wreckage myself and I was sad but less than when watching television, 'cause on the television everything looks more real, links are instant, the carnage comes suddenly into your home, no planning, no-one says, 'let's go to the carnage,' it's just there.

In the flesh, a few days later, the site of the carnage is full of people who watch the wreckage or watch other people who are staring into nothing.

Loads were shaking their heads talking quietly.

There were lots of pictures of the Madonna cellotaped to the trees, and some poems.

And these really long messages, hard to get, and some children's thoughts.

If I had a kid, I'd also get him to write some poems about the dead and take him to carnages.

The evening the bomb went off in Via Palestro, bombs exploded in other parts of Italy.

I changed channels to find out where.

I thought that maybe it was the end of Italy. That everything would explode.

Going to bed I kept thinking about that Moroccan guy being blown up on the bench. When you let people sleep where they want to, you can't guarantee they'll wake up the next day.

The next day I even went to a demonstration. Everybody was angry but no one managed to be angry at anyone in particular.

We were just angry in general.

I would have liked to say something to Rai Uno's interviewers, but if they'd interviewed me I wouldn't have known what to say. I would have said that you can't do this, this carnage.

Then we went to Burghy and I had a king bacon and regular fries and a cheeseburger and an orange juice and an apple strudel, while my girlfriend had a king cheeseburger and a fish burger and a small fries and a large coke

Yoghurt

It's good to buy books.

A home without books is very sad.

I've got 75 of them.

All encyclopaedias, because other books make a mess.

Many have covers in the same colour, others, like the History of Fascism or the Modern Fisherman's Encyclopaedia are in different colours.

The newsagent keeps the issues of the encyclopaedias in the colours I tell him. I put them together and put them in the house.

I, who has lots of books, am Ugo. I am 40. My zodiac sign is Pisces.

One encyclopaedia I have is the history of philosophy. If you want to read it, you have to know that to start with you understand it, and then later on you don't. At the end it's complicated. At the beginning there are some people who explain how everything is made of one thing. One says that everything is made of water, another says that everything is made of air and so on.

For me, the world is made of yoghurt and you understand this little by little, with age.

When you're a child you don't understand it, you take things without thinking about them, saving money to buy them and then you use them, you play with them without thinking about what they're made of.

The bar downstairs that stays open till three in the morning sells ice cream in different flavours.

For instance, chocolate flavour. Or vanilla. Then yoghurt. But the yoghurt is plain, apricot or in other flavours. This is because the apricot tastes of apricot, being made of apricot, but even before tasting of apricot it tastes of yoghurt because it's made of yoghurt, it's apricot yoghurt from which, afterwards, they extract the pure apricot and sell it, and so on for the other flavours and other things.

Take for instance Mulino Bianco cakes. Go and check the ingredients if you have some in your dining room. It says that they are softened with apricot yoghurt.

Before yoghurt the world was hard, full of dinosaurs and beasts explained in the encyclopaedia of prehistoric animals. Men did not eat yoghurt and were completely stupid.

They were beast-like. Little by little they understood that it's useless to fight, because everything is made of yoghurt. Everything is the same and it's not worth getting too upset about things. This is the history of philosophy properly explained.

I think that not everyone (almost no one) knows this. To know this you would have to buy books that help you to think, not only pornographic magazines and women's romances, because they are, yes, made of yoghurt like everything else, but they are hard, prehistoric, they talk about other things altogether and you don't realise how things really work, you go out in the squares to demonstrate with the Communists, you don't buy yoghurt anymore, you buy Galbani desserts, you eat them without thinking what they are really made of, you get further and further away from yoghurt, the years go by and in the course of existence nothing changes, you go through life just like that, good for nothing, until you die and turn into yoghurt again.

Argentina Brasile Africa

Now how am I going to tell my wife, and how can I ring her to tell her when we still have three years of mortgage to pay on the house and two years of loan, tatatattà

For the car. Now I'm going to park it here in the middle of Piazza Loreto. Now I'm going to park it here now. That I have no hope of doing anything for my children's future now that

It's raining so hard the car near the petrol station, yes... I don't think I could have this feeling of blood pumping so hard, of fear now that

My name is Luigi. I'm twenty eight.
  I've been sacked and this rain, this evening, is so sweet and so wet now. I've got to phone Bertoni to tell him I need to give him the office keys. Now that

It's raining in Piazza Argentina I remember that

My mother, when I was young, used to tell me (it's crazy I'm remembering this now) my mother would tell me that every drop that falls on the ground or on the ledges of Motta or anywhere is a thought that evaporates, and goes back to the earth.

I don't know what will happen to me tomorrow, the day after tomorrow I need to reorganise my existence, I need to know what

Will happen to my children if I can keep the house I share in Palau, now…

Now. I'm getting out of the car. Now that it's raining I'm getting out cause this rain is making me cry because now I have a moment of time to look at it to feel it trickle down my face on my

Cardigan as if I've never had time to notice it and feel it running down my hands now I'm taking my dick out of my trousers in the middle of Corso Buenos Aires I'm taking

My dick out of my trousers without an umbrella getting out in front of the entrance of Lima Station without pulling on my raincoat now

That it is raining I want to knock myself out.
     For once I want to totally knock myself out here and then go up towards Piazza
     ARGENTINA as if
     BRASILE and as if all of
     AFRICA now under this rain were hugging me under this

Rain were hugging me and enough of this chaos as if I were on a ledge as if soon

I were to dissolve in this rain that rains today Wednesday 24th January soon I will no longer exist because I am now getting out of the car like this and every drop that is falling now every drop that

is falling now.

Translated from the Italian by
Zoe Lambert and Sara D'Orazio

Once in a Lifetime, Man, and After That, Y'Know, F'getit

Dalibor Šimpraga

'Tween us, man, I fuck'd some twenny-thir'y cunts, to sum'em all, like, up. No shit, man. An' all in all, I always chased them down. But, y'know, in truth, it was them fuckin' chasin' me down. Y'know, I always play it safe, like, as Špriher says, I'd call it only with two pair. If chance's slim, you don't even start thinkin' and it's closin' time, man, no matter if she's centrefold material. An' that's what happen'd with Ines, really. Y'know, at first I was not even in love with her. Y'see, goin' to the textile high, pussy's available for export, like, wagonful of pussy, y'know, just pick an' choose, like in that kraut home shoppin' catalogue with 500 pages. An' so, one day, as I drop in for some schoolin', a chick from downstairs hall tells me there's this junior chick interested in me. An' I go: »*As if any's not interested*«, tha's me, ridin' all high-an'-mighty, like, arrogant, y'know, seventeen and top of the fuckin' world, like them squirts in trams today, drivin' everybody nuts. Fuckit, at least we carried no scruffy backpacks, like, fuck'em all, if I met myself as seventeen t'day, I'd kick myself in the ass, y'know, or if I'd a bro in high school now, I'd beat the crap out of him. OK, where was I, ah, yeah — she says: Fila, if you're so cool, at least come to the cafeteria, y'know, tomorrow at recess, to meet her, y'know, I feel kinda sorry for the girl, she,

63

like, totally flipped for you. An' I seen Ines at recess before, seemed too ordinary though, y'know, but, I say – *let's do this and all, may as well get a free soda*. So, next day I come to the cafeteria, them two by the window. An' Ines all made up, fuckit, had some red dress on, y'know, kinda velvety, and dark blue tights and flats. Man, I fell like a possum. Fuck, if I saw a broad dress'd like that now, I'd make her out a country gal or somethin', but then, fuckit, then as if she leap'd right out of a fuckin' magazine, y'know, *haute* fashion. I fuckin' drooled, like, aw, she's so hot and all that jazz. An' me, a sweet talkin' creep I was, better 'en anybody, big words an' all, so in no time we have a date after school. An' so, we meet, like, chat for an hour or two, she just eyein' me wide, I say to myself, lemme snag a smooch, nothin' to lose. An' we, like, french kiss, y'know, Bogart an' all, can't believit. That evenin' we roam the streets like a normal couple, y'know, ice cream an' all, chitchat, gossipin' on some stupid cows from my class, plannin' for the New Year's party and so.

An' fuckit, broke up after a week. Hell if I know why, somethin' stupid, what else. No calls for two days, I fuckin' wait like on the death row, y'know, as if electrocuted, can't sit on my ass for a second, but I won't call first, no way, José. Can't stay at home, I toss an' turn, go outside, again no place holds me, so I go back home, y'know, maybe she's called. Ask mom, whatever, somethin', if Igor, like, called. She says nobody called. Me a fuckin' puddle on the floor, a total meltdown. Like, a calamity in slow motion, helpless, angry, bitter, with no idea for revenge. An' more, then I fuckin' picture her with her ex, goin' out, goin' back to his place, him fuckin' her, then I make lists of debutantes to cheat back at her, an' all that. *Derangitis myelitis*, as Žmarac'd say. Then she calls first. Like, »*Drazen, can't live without you, everything's pointless*«, and she's so chirpin' like a canary, makes you cry. An' I go, »*Sweety tweety, c'mon, let's get t'gether, y'know*

I'm not mad at you«, I sing oh-so-sweetly. An' she goes: »*And, where?*«, y'know, I still get fuckin' goosebumps 'bout how nice it was then. Like, violins, *save yer love, mah dahlin'*... She goes: »*Old place, then?*« Y'know, city centre, main square, next to the tobacconist's. The *old fuckin' place*, like as if we'd dated for five years and not a week; still, fuckit, y'know how it goes. An' so, we wanna screw righ' away, but have nowhere to go. Fuckit, so cold outside, end of the fuckin' year, like, penguins linin' up for Caribbean visas. I say, »*Ines, what the fuck we care, let's fuck anywhere*«, I mean, that's not what I said, but it was the idea, so we end up somewhere in the fuckin' outskirts, on Ksaver, some new hillside fancy block, near a church, some benches between the hedgerows, no-one in sight, snow all 'round, all peace and quiet, fuckin' Antarctica, I'm tellin' ya. I mean, no-one in sight, yeah, right, no corner in this city with fuckin' no-one in sight. An' lissen to what fuckin' happens next. She's sittin' in my lap, like, bliss an' all, it's freezin' cold and my dick goin' in-out, feelin' just right, y'know, as it's wet, ya' feel the cold on it, so ya' push it back deep inside, fuckin' heaven, man, we fuck an' fuck, when a rotweiller jumps out of the bushes, walks over to us, sniffin' us y'know where. Ines scared shitless, yeah, I lost my cool, too, man, the pecker at fuckin' ease, curfew time, y'know, the fuck's over now. Then this dude appears, shoutin', callin' »Ara! Ara!«, pretendin' not to see us, but grinnin', ya' get the idea, right? Fuckit, the dude leaves, we dress up, like, headin' home. But, fuckit, I wanna fuck, she wanna fuck. I say: »*Tweety sweety, let's go back for a li'l while*«, she'd hardly wait. Like, that time, y'know, that secon' fuck, that time I screw'd 'er as never before or after, like, as Špriher says, *I felt the golden vein in it.*

Y'know, fuck me an' all, but all those other cunts I screw'd after Ines were nothin', man. I guess I was in love with her only. But, whassit, a year, just around the anniversary, as a Bosnian from work says: *lovinversary*, when I figur'd the shit out. She fuckin' went to Sarajevo, trainin' for the openin' of the

Universiad Games, the creep must've made her up there. An' how I find out, Sherlock fuckin' Holmes. Us bein' the same school shifts an' all, swappin' notebooks at recess to write fuckin' love messages, y'know. So I open her notebook at the back, nothin' special, but one page torn out, man. An' there, a fuckin' imprint on the blank page, y'know. An' me, y'know, no fuckin' rest 'till I find out what she wrote and tore, so I take a pencil and shade all over the imprint, y'know, like when we clone'd coins in kiddie school. Yeah, right, she wrote a note to some fuckin' Bruno that she can't come that afternoon, 'cause of who the fuck cares what. An' me, fuckit, feelin' as that redneck from my army squad'd say: »*Cut me in two, righ'ere*«. After school, a fuckin' zero. I say nuthin', play dumb, but she gets it, like, somethin's wrong. Y'know, cunts hate it more when ya' keep stumm, then when ya' fuckin' holler at 'em. She goes, like, »*Dražen, what's the matter?*«, I go »*Nuthin'*« and all that. Then at the gate she exits while I pass thru the hole in the schoolyard fence. She goes »*Why do you go thru the fence?*«, an' I go: to push my horns thru, that some Bruno gave me. She breaks into tears. Like, sobs an' all, nuthin's her fault, an' all that, y'know, chick talk. She starts tellin' me, like, everythin', where the creep lives, where he goes to school, like, but they're friends, y'know, met him at the Games, as if I still fuckin' cared: maybe there's nuthin' 'tween them, y'know, not my fuckin' problem no more, *arriverderci signorina*. Just fuckin' imagine me, man. Like, I fuckin' know it's, as Džudi says, *game over*, nuthin' to be done no more. Lemme tell ya, man, it took me half a year to come 'round. But, OK, better that, y'know, than this scenario: *ah, you have a date,* y'know. *And I thought we might go see that American movie tonight.* Or, like, *D. F., twentyeight yrs. old, father of two underage children, stabs himself then wife to death with a screwdriver*. Like, neighbours say they've never heard of such a crime.

Translated from the Croatian by Tatjana Jambrišak

ATHENS

The Four Hundred Pleats

AMANDA MICHALOPOULOU

By the end of my studies I was acting like a true Brit. I ate baked beans for breakfast, called my roommate 'my lovely,' and every Saturday would go to Harrods and buy some small, useless object. The olives I had bought in a fit of nostalgia rotted in their glass jar in the halls of residence refrigerator, behind a label that read *Authentic Greek Olives.*

In the afternoons, as the sun set as slowly and dramatically as a Turner seascape, I gazed out the window of my low-ceilinged room onto the red brick of the neighbouring halls of residence and the jagged chimneys in the background. I would smoke the day's last cigarette sitting by the window with its broken latches and the crusted bird droppings on the sill, and dream of living in London forever. I had no real reason to return to Athens. My friends had scattered to private universities all across Europe and the U.S. And my parents could live without me.

After I handed in my Masters thesis, I shut myself up in halls. I inhaled the damp of my room; I caressed the carpet, whose nap was pockmarked with cigarette burns, and I packed my suitcases, picking up my clothes one article at a time, carefully folding each. The sky had taken on its characteristic leaden colour. I remembered the soldier from the fairy tale, the one with the leaden heart. Now I had grown up and become that soldier. A mercenary in the Legion of Foreign Students. A Master in Art History.

I returned home. My parents both worked — to put me through college, as they often reminded me — at an advertising agency. Thanks to the agency, they had got wrapped up in the upcoming Olympics. The house was full of hats and mugs bearing the Olympic logo. They came home at night so tired they would forget words. 'Where'd you get the thingumybob,' they'd say, or 'Have you seen the whatsit?' My father had given up football. The only time he really cheered like a sports fan now was when they landed big jobs at the office. My mother even forgot my birthday.

I didn't know what to do with myself back at home, how to behave in my parents' house. It seemed gloomy to me, smaller and stuffier than my attic room in halls had been. I rung round all my old friends, in alphabetical order. Half of them were still in school. The other half worked all day like my parents, and didn't have time for me anymore. I kept hoping someone I knew would come up to me in the street and say, 'Hey! What are you doing here?' But the only people who paused at all were tourists looking for a bank, or for the entrance to the monorail that would take them to the top of Lycavittos.

It was July when I first saw him. The sun, lifeless in the sky, bathed all of Athens in its light. I had walked as far as the National Gardens in search of a patch of shade. There was a depressing little zoo there with some chickens and ducks and a few ostriches that seemed to be suffering from the heat. They reminded me of myself: I too was tall and out of place in my surroundings. On my way home I passed by Parliament, dragging my feet, eyes on the ground. So I saw his shoes first, with their funny pompoms. Then the white leggings of his summer uniform, the pleats of his skirt — the traditional foustanela, blindingly white in the sun — his bayonet, his well-polished gun. His chest was wide and strong under his fermeli. His face was the most beautiful thing I had ever seen: eyes as green as the olives I had left to rot, a long, thin nose, velvety lips, and a vein in his left temple that bulged as if it were carved from stone.

A few giggling tourists had gathered around him. They wore baggy shorts and their toes were coated with dust from all the construction taking place for the Olympics. I stood a little way off, turned my head and watched him from an angle. His eyes met mine with that harsh, severe look they must learn during basic training. It was love at first sight for us both.

I passed whole days in front of Parliament, living on water and koulouria I bought from street vendors, like the backpack-laden tourists. Eventually I learned his shifts. Three times a day, for five hours at a time, he would stand straight-backed and motionless under his awning, and on the half-hour would dance his peculiar dance. Morning, noon, and night I watched those slapping steps with his funny shoes, the sleight of hand with his bayonet. The rest of the time he was forbidden to move — but there was no way they could control the movements of his eyes. Beneath the merciless sun he watched me, never batting an eye.

I spoke to him in a low monotone, so the other soldiers wouldn't notice. Moving my mouth as little as possible, with little twitches and spasms, I told him about myself: 'Do you want to know what I was studying? Art history, contemporary art. I know everything about the Neurotic Realists — I'm probably even more neurotic than them. Somehow I grew to hate Athens; I don't remember why. Maybe it was the pollution, before the advent of unleaded petrol? All the bureaucracy? History class in school? The way people drive like maniacs? You know, the first thing you learn in London is to circulate invisibly through the crowds. You have to keep your face blank, even if they hold you down and pull out your nails one at a time. An 'ouch' or two will suffice. But isn't that what you do, too? The evzone, guardian of history! I bet if I bit you you wouldn't scream.' I kneeled down and sank my teeth into his thigh. His blood stained his white tights but my evzone didn't let out a peep.

Another time I said: 'I had to get away from here, you know? Not for my studies, really — just to stop being myself, to try being someone else for a change. One way was to eat baked beans for breakfast. Another was to wash my clothes at the launderette in my neighbourhood, near Euston Station. Have you ever been to London? Do you know what it means to cry in the rain? And now I can't decide which I like better, England or Greece, the old wallpaper printed with coats of arms or our old family home in Kineta. But I know I like you. I like you a lot. And you're the Greekest thing there is, right?' When my evzone agreed, he would blink his eyes. When he disagreed he would look at me dispassionately like a tired man on the subway, or a psychoanalyst.

Then one evening in the second month of our acquaintance, everything changed.

The sky was as blue as in touristy postcards from the islands. It was August 15th — the Assumption of Mary, day of miracles — and a north wind was blowing. The branches of the trees on Vassilisis Sophia bent gently but firmly toward the pavement. The breeze also seemed to blow through my head, clearing my thoughts.

'I'm in love with you,' I told my evzone. 'But I'm not entirely sure what you are to me. When I want you, you become my God. When I'm angry you look like you're wearing a costume. Right now you look like a beautiful white object. Even the way you hold your bayonet... how can I describe it? You make me feel like it's all just an image. You're just a guard with a fancy fermeli and no feelings, that's all. You're even more hypocritical than the Brits: your foot falls asleep so you start dancing around like Karaghiozis; you want to follow me but stand there gaping. What kind of a man are you, anyway?'

'I'm not a man right now. I'm not a hundred percent

man,' my evzone whispered, blushing bright red for the first time. 'I'm an idea.'

'Bullshit.'

'My foustanela has four hundred pleats. One for each year of the Ottoman Occupation.'

'So you're still afraid of the Turks? Jesus, can't you live without enemies?'

'Right now you're my worst enemy,' he said sadly.

'So leave your post. Comfort me. Make your famous idea more human.'

'They'll discipline me.'

'So what?' I said, with the stubbornness of a lover who requires constant proofs of love.

'I don't know if this will work. Between us, I mean.'

'So what? Look around you. It's August and everyone's white as a sheet. They all work till they're ready to drop. I've been waiting around all this time. And what am I asking? Just for you to take me on a walk, or a ride.'

'Find a bike.'

'What?'

'A bike, I said. A motorcycle.'

I stood in the middle of Vassilisis Sophias and pulled a girl off her motorbike. She fought back. I jerked her hair, bit her arm. I whistled to my evzone. He hopped onto the seat, and I hung on behind him. He turned the key in the ignition and we jumped forward. There were two police cars right on our tail, but my evzone, in a single, graceful movement, pulled out his bayonet and slashed their tyres. He ran all the red lights and we ducked into the narrow sidestreets of Plaka, which were full of parked cars. It smelled of fried cod. When he turned off the engine we could hear the police sirens more clearly.

'You're crazy,' I said, and hugged him.

'No, there's just something I want to show you.' We pushed the motorbike into a little yard off a quiet lane in

Anafiotika. We rolled it behind a staircase and moved a few oil drums potted with basil to hide it. With his bayonet he cut the rope off a wooden swing and shoved it under his vest. His tights had got dirty, and the pompom on one of his shoes was dangling like a bad tooth. As for the four hundred pleats, they had got completely squashed.

'So much for the Ottoman Empire,' I chuckled.

My evzone shot me a stern glance, then nodded for me to follow him. When we reached the base of the Holy Rock he took the rope out of his vest, tied it to the tip of his bayonet, made a few knots, and we started our upward climb. He would stick the bayonet into crevices in the rock, we'd step on the knots to climb up, then search for jutting rocks to stand on while he pulled out the bayonet and wedged it in a little higher. By the time we reached the Parthenon the sun was gone from the sky. The columns were lit up at night like the teeth of some mythic beast. My evzone had ripped his dress on the climb, but he was more beautiful and angrier than ever.

I was angry, too. I was angry at everything: at the beauty and the breeze, at the cicadas' monotonous cries, at the girl on her motorbike for fighting back, at the police for intervening, at the fact that my evzone wasn't perfect.

'What did you want to show me?'

He took one of my cigarettes, lit it, and sat down cross-legged at the edge of the rock.

'See there, in the distance? That's where I live. See that lighted window? Not that building, with the pool on the terrace — what kind of family do you think we are? A little to the left, in that apartment building, the one with seven storeys. My parents must be eating. My brother will be reading comic books. They fight over which channel to watch; they don't have money for a second TV.'

'We have three. Want one of ours?'

'They wouldn't accept. My mother may go to the

market with an empty wallet, but she never leaves the house
without lipstick. As for my father...'

'What?'

'He's aged. He doesn't see well anymore. He holds his
newspaper upside-down.'

'Is your brother older or younger?'

'Younger. He's terrified they'll make him be an evzone,
too. He's even taller than I am. He has three piercings in his
ear and one in his nose.'

'That's no good. Your energy seeps out those holes, you
know.'

'And that's exactly what drives me crazy. The holes, the
lost energy, the comics.'

'You're so old-fashioned...'

'No, I'm just what I am.'

'What are you?'

He dropped his cigarette in the dirt and ground it out
with his shoe.

'I brought you here so you could see for yourself what I
am.'

He opened his arms and I burrowed into his embrace. It
was a large white embrace that smelled of green soap and
mothballs. I tried to pull off his shoes and tights. I tugged at
his foustanela. My evzone didn't resist. On the contrary, he
encouraged me, taking my face in his hands and kissing it
gently with his frozen lips. But the fabrics were very stiff, like
marble, and seemed stuck to his skin. I grabbed hold of his
bayonet, I fondled him through his tights — but all I felt was
the cold wind of history.

'Why are you doing that?' I asked.

'I told you, I'm not a hundred percent man.'

I was more in love, more desperate than ever. I didn't
believe him; I had seen the red stain on his tights when I bit
him. I knew he could be a man if he wanted to.

'You're driving me—' I said, panting.

'Come on, let's try again,' he said. He undid the top button of his shirt and I tugged again at the fabric. The little patch of exposed skin was red and hot. Soon it was covered with blisters. It smelled burnt.

My evzone turned the other way. I couldn't tell if he was in pain or if he just wanted to be alone for a while. He lit another cigarette and looked at me sadly.

'You're right,' I said. 'There's nothing doing with us.'

He set about straightening his pleats, almost obsessively. Four hundred pleats, one by one. It took him a long time. The cigarette dangled from his lips. Ash fell, until nothing was left but the filter. The sky grew dark and the cicadas told their stories. Bit by bit I forgot I had been angry with him.

'You're a strange girl,' he said at last.

'You're strange, too. You behave like some folk philosopher.'

'What you see is what you get.'

'What kind of music do you listen to?'

'It depends on the situation.'

'That's not an answer. What's your favourite food?'

'Okra.'

'Ew. All that slime.'

'Well, what's your favourite food, baked beans?'

'Whatever I feel like.'

We sat side by side all night long, smoking. Every so often I would ask my evzone a question. He would answer fairly willingly, and then ask me the same question. What was my favourite book, my favourite male name — stupid stuff like that. I couldn't answer a single one. It was like I wasn't sure of anything anymore. All my preferences, all my tastes had been erased. I was exhausted from lack of sleep and my inability to decide made me cranky.

'You're the phoniest person in the world,' I finally said to him. I was angry with him for pretending to accept life as it was. He was pretending to be wise and important. I felt like thinking up three hundred and ninety nine more insults. One for each of his pleats.

'You're malicious. Ill-bred. A bully.'

My evzone stood up and walked to the edge of the rock.

'Conservative. Reactionary. Antagonistic.'

The sun burst like a bloody wound in the sky.

'Arrogant. Cynical. Didactic.'

My evzone spread his arms and flapped them back and forth like wings.

'Lazy. Egocentric. Jealous.'

He dived with a tumble into the void. His foustanela spread like a fan around his body. The four hundred pleats rustled. He flew with strong, broad, masculine strokes, like a champion swimmer. I looked at him with envy, with desire. At the same time I understood that I had let him down, too, and there was no way he was coming back. And then I saw the pompom from his shoe glistening in the first rays of the morning sun. It had fallen on the ground where we had been lying. I picked it up and clenched my fist around it. Then I grabbed my arm and bit it, until blood ran.

Translated from the Greek by Karen Emmerich

PRAGUE

The News and Views

EMIL HAKL

1)

At around ten I swung by the bank to see if by any chance any money had come in. 'Ya got twoooo thousin' five hundrid,' said the clerk. 'That's too bad,' I feigned disappointment. 'OK, I'll take the two thousand.' I took the money and went directly to the butcher's shop. There were three female assistants standing behind the counter. I was looking at the iridescent bright red tendons, lined up regiments of pink cutlets, white sheets of bacon, capriciously rolled up red gristles, klobasas, salamis, and rough beef tongues smoked to a copper colour. Hanging from hooks were pork knuckles, hunks of smoked meat and ribs like blinds in a window.

A smooth male voice on the radio recited the news, 'A human arm wrapped in plastic was found in a garbage container in the District of Prague 6, and according to the initial police report belonged either to a young woman or a juvenile...'

'*Grosssss!*' shouted all three assistants spontaneously.

'...the police therefore ask residents who may have noticed anything suspicious during the specified period,' the velvety voice smoothly continued, 'to immediately contact...'

'May I help you?' asked the youngest.

'This turkey breast over here, about a kilo please,' I pointed.

The girl tossed the meat on the scale and twittered, 'Is two kilos too much?'

'That's too much, could you cut some off?' I said.

'How's this?'

I nodded.

The butcher swiped the chunk of meat from which she easily separated the tip, slapped it on the scale, and I gave her the money.

Back home I cut the meat thinly, added salt, pepper, thyme and rosemary, placed the slices in a pan with hot oil and put potatoes and broccoli on to boil next to it. The kitchen sizzled and steamed and the world behind the window got to be one shade brighter.

'Damn, that sure smells good!' came a voice from the corridor.

2)

At around three thirty it started to snow lightly. I found myself standing with a full stomach at Charles Square beside the Eliška Krásnohorská statue, waiting to go for a bit of a walk with Mikeš. After a while I started pacing to warm up a bit. Eliška's eyes were like boiled eggs and were more and more resembling a newt in formaldehyde.

'Would you happen to have a cigarette?' uttered someone into my ear.

A woman in her mid twenties was standing there.

'Last two, I'm sorry.'

'Aren't you gonna buy some more?'

'I'm in my thrifty period, you know.'

'I do,' she nodded. She had astonishingly honest, pure eyes. And a strange, sped-up diction. She spoke as if at the beginning of each sentence she was throwing herself into the darkness amongst monsters. As if she was working her way through a dark forest. And her curly hair splashed about her round face.

It made me reach into my pocket, 'All right, I got six of 'em here, help yourself.'

She had me light it up for her.

'Beautiful snow,' she pointed to the sky with her cigarette.

'You bet, I'm glad.'

'Me, too, but it's cold. Got a little date here?'

'I'm meeting a buddy.'

The woman nodded. She was wearing knitted leggings. A skirt. A little jacket. A scarf around her neck. I was thinking what else I could say. A freshly completed glass box was towering above the crossroads.

'I don't mind when they put up new buildings,' I said.

'Me neither,' she said.

'I didn't even mind when they blew up the old Tatra factory in Smíchov and built Carrefour there instead. But that,' I pointed to the building, 'that is too much!'

'Think so?' She re-examined the cube. 'Yeah, it's horrible.'

'Super-horrible,' I added.

'It's freezing cold,' she shivered. 'When it's this cold it's best to climb under a duvet, huh?'

'I don't think so.'

'And a bit of sex too...'

'Oh, forget about sex,' I droned and blew my nose for no particular reason.

'So what else in this weather?'

'Well, like I said, a walk with a buddy, a couple of beers and home.'

'As you wish... But I would do it to you good, for four hundred. Or three, you're pretty nice.'

'No really, thanks.'

The woman shuffled her foot and tapped the ash off her cigarette. It was obvious that she hadn't slept around that much, but for some reason she really needed the money. Her irises looked as if they were composed of two transparent light-brown layers. One could travel in them. I was switching from background to foreground and felt like that celluloid ship that goes back and forth in a promotional pen.

'So two hundred then?' she said.

'No really, I'd rather just chat with you over coffee but there's no time.'

A text message vibrated in my pocket: *Sorry, sick, in bed, wolfing down some ham from Pavlína, and watching Crime Site Munich. Let's do walk another time. M.*

Where are we, I thought to myself. Where are we and what the hell are we doing here!? Whatever happened to goofing around? Lately we've just been rattling our mouths over and over, bitching about the same things and laughing at the same things, where's the humour? What happened to those times we drank all night and took in a bunch of rock and roll and then went to work in the morning? Now we just go for walks and rattle our traps, and even that's no fun anymore!

'The little date's not happening, eh?' she remarked jovially.

'No, my buddy's watching TV.'

'I'd also like to watch TV.'

'How about a coffee then?' I asked her.

'Really?' she said suggestively, 'or how about going over to your buddy's to watch TV?'

'He lives far away.'

He didn't, but like I said.

'I knooow already,' she whined. 'So let's meet in the café over there, all right? I'll just take care of some business here and then catch up with you,' her teeth chattered and she disappeared into an underpass. A minute later she was happily showing me a little plastic package hidden in her hand. 'Don't you want some, too? I could go get you some, but you'd have to put up some cash for it.'

'No, no,' I waved my arm and felt a noticeable cranial kind of desire just like the urge to scratch oneself where a scab used to be. 'I gave that up a long time ago.'

3)

'I got it under control this,' she assured me after we sat down, 'I don't even inject it, you knooow...'

I nodded.

'Yep, a little line now and then and that's that,' she said and averted her eyes.

'Hm.'

'You're not using anything?' she asked.

'Why?'

'Just 'cause, everyone's using something...'

'I just have some mushrooms once in a while and that's enough for me.'

'So what's it like, mushrooms, is it a sort of an *upper*?' she inquired.

'Not exactly, it's sort of pretty clean...'

'Like what do you mean?'

'Compared to this crap it's much more peaceful.'

'And you get smashed on this *every day*?'

'Oh no, not at all, once in three months me and a couple of buddies drive into the woods, away from people, eat it there, lie on the moss until the evening, then sleep over in a sleeping bag. In the morning pick up our shit and get going... The last time was in September, when we dragged ourselves up Milá Mountain in the Středohoří Highlands where it's so beautiful as it is anyway that we felt bad to be using anything in addition: hundred-year-old ivy-covered trees, stones overgrown with moss, and up there on the peak a green carpet of wormwood, just like a little Japanese garden... So we ate it and waited. And this one buddy – he used to be a dentist – all of a sudden grew restless and kept saying, 'I don't feel a thing, do you? I don't! It's weak! It's not working! Do you feel anything?' And I was afraid that he was gonna spoil it with his restlessness, that it wasn't gonna work the way it should because of his chatter, so it occurred to me to distract him. 'Vítek, since you used to be a dentist, would you mind having a look at my gums, I think I got some sort of inflammation there, what do you think, should I have it checked?''

'Did he quit dentistry 'cause he was tired of looking people in their gobs?' she asked.

'He quit because his colleagues in the field made him sick because they're apparently a bunch of mafia hogs. He insists he has known a lot of those who drill perfectly healthy teeth just so that they could milk some more money out of people... And so Vítek looked in my mouth and said, 'What the hell is this here? I've never seen anything like that before! How long have you had it?' 'A few months,' I said. 'Man oh man! This is the first time I've seen something like this! If I were you, I'd have it checked right away...' So I was panicked, of course, the first thing I thought of was *cancer*!'

'Haw, haw,' she giggled.

'I was about to close my mouth, but he shouted, 'Hang on, hang on, hold it up this way, I gotta have a look at this, this is *interesting*!' and the other buddy joined him and both of them were staring in my mouth on top this Milá Mountain, bug-eyed, saying, 'This is strange! What could it be, my oh my? So purple! Orange! So in-teres-ting! I haven't seen anything like this my whole life!' And I stood there, perhaps ten minutes, looking in the sun, holding my lip and showing them my gums until I realized that this was not about my trap! Their gawking had finally got things started and my trap opened some sort of tunnel into another world for them...'

The woman stared at me wide-eyed.

'Really?' she said in amazement.

'Hang on, just a sec, I'm telling you this for fun, it's really just a banal story...'

'I understaaand,' she said and kept looking at me as if I had two heads, 'so what happened then, tell me!'

'Well, then all three of us finally got it going, so we lay in the grass and observed how the humming of the whole countryside gradually made its way to us. And then I suddenly heard this sound, as if a helicopter had turned its engine on next to my head, *vshu vshu vshu vshu*, so I jumped up and looked to see what was happening. And it was a brimstone butterfly that flew by...'

'Huh!' shouted the woman and grabbed the table, almost toppling it over and looking just swell.

'What's going on?' I asked.

'Nothing, it's just that you still haven't told me what it's like, mushrooms.'

'Quick or slow, it depends on where you are. In any case you experience that everything's pulsating, that everything's just waves on different frequencies, words, space, colours, it all falls apart and then comes back together like some Lego. You experience all the ticking and rattle that you consist of, there's no matter, just a silent agreement amongst the molecules... You simply take a peek behind the curtain and it makes no difference from which side; you can have a blast and it can be deadly, but you can't take any of that back with you. Everything stays there...'

'I know.'

'I bet you do.'

'Know what, I'm gonna just sort of step out a bit and maybe have another java with milk,' she said, and walked away toward the back somewhere wiggling her ass, not that she wanted to, but she just was that way.

A minute later she danced in wearing those leggings like

mama's little treasure at a school open house. Her nose spattered with freckles. Pupils like two plates.

'So where are you frommm anyways?' she asked when she sat down.

'Me, from here, Prague, and you?'

'Probably from a different planet, some place really far away,' she said and smiled. And behind that smile I caught a glimpse of the kind of weariness not known by those who slave from nine to five and fill the air with talk and buzzing and have their radios on loud at the same time, and then go home for dinner, because they are the main reason for that weariness.

'But I have no place to live here, which is sort of pretty bad,' she added absentmindedly.

'So, where do you sleep in this weather?'

'I've just said that I have no place to live, right ... But I do have like a place in Prípotocní Street, a little plaaace... The trouble is that I can't stand being alone, you know, there's always someone staying over, the last time I lived with a guitar player, a young jerk in leather, I don't know at all what I saw in him. He was as good looking as a skinned orangutan, but sometimes he was nice to me, you don't need much, right. The heart is stupid...'

'Yeah. And where did he play?' I asked.

'That's the thing, he didn't play anywhere because he was a troublemaker, when he drank he acted up. Other than that he was cool. It's just that he always wanted to sort of change me. When I'd tell him something he looked at me like... what's the word?'

'Vile? Vicious?'

'*Vile* is nonsense and I didn't mean *vicious*, he looked at me *hatefully* like what I was saying was idiotic and boring. And when I was silent, he smashed things and blamed me saying this was no life not talking to each other, that it pissed him off when not even that tap would speak to him. So I asked him, 'So what do you wanna talk about? Tell me and we'll talk!' And he shouted, 'Don't know, how the fuck should I know! I don't know!'

'It's like that everywhere, people live beside each other and they're afraid to keep going and they're even more afraid to end it,' I said.

'I know, but this started to get really sort of shitty. He started to stare at me strangely, didn't speak, listened to the Ramštjans cranked all the way up and was as pleasant as water in the stomach, you know. I knew him, so I knew he was nuts and that he was positively gonna do something. And do something he did. Once he got up at night, I was sleeping like a pimpernel...'

'Like a pimpernel?'

'Yeah, sleeping like a pimpernel, he must've put some shit in my drink, some fucking sleeping pill, because I didn't wake up when he was tattooing me...'

'Tattooing?'

'Yeah, he tattooed me all over, he had a tattoo gun.'

'Really?'

'Yeah, he wrote all over me and took off. Look.' She rolled up her sleeve and showed me a row of thin bluish letters, that spread unevenly across the top of her arm: THE LEFT ARM OF A SLUT.

'My legs, look.' She pulled up her skirt and rolled down her leggings. Good thing we were sitting in the corner. White thighs with fine dark hair on it appeared: THE RIGHT LEG OF A SLUT. THE LEFT LEG OF A SLUT.

'And look over here,' she pulled down her skirt and hiked up her sweater and t-shirt. I saw an alabaster stomach. Her navel looked out at me from under its smooth, somewhat swollen eyelids. I LOVE YOU! was written right above the navel in an arc as if it had an eyebrow. FUCK ME! I'LL GO TO HELL! was written on the opposite side below the navel, also in an arc, but upside down. And below that something of a line downwards.

'Watcha got there?'

'This is sort of an arrow,' she said.

I felt a sweet longing in the nether regions. Unwittingly I remembered the legend about a painter who was painting the Devil; the Devil showed himself to him in parts because if the painter had seen him completely, he would have been done for then and there.

'And look at this,' she showed me a tiny diamond shape on the upper edge of the pelvis and then quickly hid it again. I noticed a comic speech bubble rising from the diamond shape and in it was a word, but I didn't have time to read it.

'I'LL HOLD IT UP FOR ANYONE, it says on my butt, but that's not true at all...,' she whined. 'And the places you'd sort of ask about anyway he skipped over, otherwise I'd probably have woken up... Only here,' she pulled down the collar of her sweater and revealed the upper part of her defiantly shaped breast. There was a skinny saw-toothed little figure with a circle with two holes for a head, crosshatched trunk and four lines, arms, legs. Above the figure was written: FAREWELL! and below WE'RE ALL GONNA DIE ANYWAY.

'That's the only one I can agree with,' she commented matter-of-factly. 'When I get some money, I'll have the lines removed, and maybe this one I'll keep. Do you know where they do this kind of removal?'

'Dunno. Once I had a tattoo on my back, but a few weeks later it got inflamed and drained out by itself.'

'That's what I would really need now.'

'Right. But what about that guitar player?'

'What about him, I haven't seen him since.'

The woman leaned her head against the back of her hand and suddenly a quick tear slid down her cheek.

'It's all falling apart for me,' she sighed. 'What am I doing here, such a simple question, and I don't even know that... What the hell am I doing here?'

'Nobody knows.'

'But I think to myself more and more that I'd be glad if those terrorist dudes just blew it all up here, the War of the Worlds, you know what I mean! Because anything's better than this day-by-day stuff.'

'I wouldn't be glad,' I said and listened to the sugar quietly pouring from side to side in the elongated baggie I took from the saucer. 'Because I think it would be more fair if it all fell apart by itself, without anybody's help, and it's falling apart already anyway.'

'I love coffee, I love tea...,' she hummed, 'but it won't be that way.'

'Why do you think so?'

'Because we're living only sort of in our thoughts, you know, we're so out of it that we're not strong enough to clear out the parade while we can... We're living only on words... Someone's got to help us!'

'I could only respond to that with words.'

'Well words, go ahead and say them... all my pals that managed to get themselves out of this shit-hole suddenly started to sort of *believe*, and they got words for everything... supposedly they learned something about themselves they didn't know in one moment of truth, and therefore they will be *forgiven*...'

'What shit-hole?'

'Doesn't matter, this involves all of us, right, *forgiven*, what kind of bullshit is that? Forgiven by whooom? For two hundred thousand years we've been wading through shit, and keep hoping that someone's gonna forgive us... Who?'

I caressed her hand.

'And stop caressing me,' she said hastily, 'or no, caress me...'

I was rolling the bag of sugar in my fingers; it felt like holding a fat and light caterpillar. I squished it and it burst. How could it be that an ordinary slut from Charles Square...

or isn't she a slut? How could it be that she can define it better than all those university graduates with two degrees?

I poured the sugar in my cup. A stray fly landed on the table and started to clean its front legs. The woman gently pushed it forward with her finger. The fly crawled forth a bit. She pushed it again. The fly crawled forth a bit again. '*Am I the last fly, bzz, bzz, my heart wants to cry,*' sang the woman.

A tall guy in his early thirties with a dyed matt black fringe carefully swept across his forehead came in the café, sat down and began to stare in the direction of our table. It's true he wasn't staring in a nosy fashion; it was like his mind wasn't there. As if he was still remembering fixing his motorbike that day.

The woman pulled up her leggings and smirked, 'Stop staring, stop staring, nincompoop!'

Dark Hair was staring and sipping his Becherovka liqueur.

'Kill the engine, you stupid moron!' the woman spoke quietly. 'Yeah, right! Dead duck!'

We chatted some more but the confidentiality of solitude was missing. The Dung Beetle kept sitting and interfering with our wavelength.

'Leave us alone and stop staring,' I said in his direction just for form. He didn't even look at me. Kept on studying the girl's small-town sweater.

'Are you insane, he could rrrrub you out,' she scolded me.

'Maybe we can still go for a bit of a walk,' I tried to salvage the pleasant early evening chitchat. 'Or we can go grab a beer some place?'

'A little stroll, that would be nice, the last person who took me for a little stroll was my fatherrrr, I'd love to go... But you know what, why don't you tell me if you're interested or not.'

'In what?'

'You know... It would be sort of pretty pleasurable.'

I shook my head.

'So we'll do a little stroll some other time, OK?' she said.

I nodded.

The woman got up and stepped out again. On her way back along that hulk's table she bent over him and whined into his ear: 'Would you have a spare cigarette for me?'

The guy looked up, staring at her as if he'd noticed her only now, and then nodded.

'Thanks,' she said and sat next to him.

The door slammed behind me and I was out. The snow was silently descending on parked cars. I looked inside through the glass. She was sitting there laughing. The dude was hunkered down, sucking his Becherovka liqueur and looked like a pumped up David Copperfield. The woman was shaking her curly head and chatting away. It looked like some horribly botched-up ending to a Christmas romance.

4)

I couldn't actually say, I thought to myself on the way, that I felt sorry for anything or anyone — myself included. But still, there's something to this way of being... Something in the way time treats material entrusted to it, or rather in the way we treat the time entrusted to us...

A man, the spitting image of the Neanderthal on a Zdenek Burián painting, stood on the tram island. He was holding a new stove pipe under his arm. It glittered in the approaching sunset as if it were alive. His white hair was blowing about over his low forehead. Beside him stood a woman with her hair cut short, compliantly watching the snowflakes disappear in a black puddle.

And women especially, I thought to myself, they take the weight of the world upon themselves at once, no talking back, many of them actually delighting in it, but none of them, excepting a few hysterical ones and exhibitionists, get all saintly about it! Women, all that's left to them is to live like saints! One saint after the other!

While contemplating I accidentally brushed against a pram going in the opposite direction.

'Watch it, you moron!' crowed the young mother.

'Kiss my ass, you stupid cow,' came out of my mouth to my own surprise.

For a moment the woman pointed her swarming crab-like periscopes at me, then presently forgot all about me.

A man on a motorcycle was charging towards me on the pavement. His rear view mirror flicked lightly, ever so lightly, against my sleeve and then was gone. I passed a few people resembling painstakingly made-up extras for a film set fifty years after a global nuclear catastrophe. A big fat blubbery broad wolfing down a potato pancake in one bite. A horribly cross-eyed man with the leg of a horse. An old Dolphin man with a smooth face free of any expression. A procession of tiny children with mean eyes and bat ears. A grandma with a small bald head and two or three wads of hair sticking out. She glanced at me, pouted her little goat-like mouth and cackled sharply.

A line-up of overcrowded trams was stuck in the street. Every five minutes one of them would always furiously ring its bell, jerk and move two metres ahead. All the others repeated the move. Behind the sweaty glass the daily inferno was taking place; bunches of bug-eyed faces were gathered there, drops of sweat were condensing, stomach ulcers were bursting and gall bladders sploshing, there was silence and there was talking in Czech, Russian, English, the iron tongues of the North, the wooden ones of the Balkans and the watery ones of the East, there was shouting in German and whispering in Ukrainian and mumbling in Hittite, Chaldean and Aramaic. And there was in fact a feeling that all these languages were seamlessly melting together and into one another and that they were returning to their original state at the time when it was more than enough to grunt, boo, hiss, sputter, howl, and produce inarticulate roaring and all-encompassing laughter.

On the embankment, a tour of physically disabled people was moving forth. In the middle of the swarm of ostentatiously, colourfully clad bodies strange hobbling, limping, hopping and shuffling was taking place. It looked liked the city had been visited by some deep-sea-dwelling languidly-flapping creature, full of jerking decoys and lures.

Two girls with braids were standing by the railing watching swans. One swan was trying to take off from the water, but wasn't having any luck because it was dragging a long piece of wire wrapped around its leg. It was flapping its wings desperately and stretching its neck out. The girls started to laugh. Then a bunch of wantonly happy disabled people swarmed over them.

At the opposite bank a fireboat painted red was lightly rocking. It's been docked there at the pier for a couple of decades, and I've never heard of it taking off into any action. Actually it did once, I remember, it's true that when the firefighters went on strike in ninety-one so that they could be called *firemen* again, they anchored their ship in front of the National Theatre and with great grandeur turned on the water canons. The polished nozzles sprayed the silver and brown Vltava waters in powerful arcs to all sides while a crowd on the embankment watched on.

I rolled up my collar, crossed the bridge and headed down the spit-covered Lidická Street into the depths of Smíchov. Before the Anděl crossroads I hung a right and carried on through the 14th of October Square. Using a crane, they were taking apart an old building resembling an ocean reef there under a floodlight behind the church. The arched alcoves and corridor holes with patterned walls were reeling in the sharp light as if alive.

5)

I walked through the deserted Kartouzská Street. Tiny snowflakes descended from the sky, and behind all this glimmering and fluttering the gigantic wall of the Carrefour supermarket loomed, with a metal bridge lit with neon from below stuck to the middle of it. I stopped for a while and looked. I felt like a tiny tourist who found himself at the foot of an overblown Egyptian tomb. And I couldn't help but see it: the fragile silver bridge even underscored a certain sick nobility of the building. Inhuman. But still noble.

A hill dusted over with white rose beyond the curve. Heck, I thought, that didn't used to be here, or did it? I stopped again and looked at an ordinary urban hill covered with bushes and trees. That's impossible, it must have been here, I thought to myself full of uncertainty. But how come I never noticed it? Could I be coming down with something? Should I just go home and take some Ibuprofen? Or am I just going nuts already?

I was so thrown off by the hill that I crossed the street, squeezed through a bush and started to climb the slope. I was walking on a path, looking under my feet and exhaling thin steam in front of me. Then I turned and took a shortcut on a steep grassy incline. The clouds ripped apart and a few stars glittered through the bare branches. *The further Genor ventured, the less lush the grass was; the hotter it was, the more noticeably the sun grew in size*, popped up in my brain out of context. *The sky was rising just a little faster than a slug* rattled in my head and squeaked like an old dictaphone, and into that I heard some urgent, ever increasing noise, but that was just ringing in my ear, *'You swine!' roared Genor, kicking her and neighing and bouncing, 'I'm a horse, I'm a horse!'*

Two tadpoles in hoodies were standing on the hill and making out below the trees. Paid no attention to me.

'Hi,' I said to them.

'Ciao,' hawked the boyo. The missy sniffed uncertainly.

'I don't mean to bug you, I just need to ask about something...' I spoke in a somewhat muted way as if in a dream. 'It just seems to me that this hill didn't used to be here before, a strange question, I know but I'm not a psycho, I just... I just feel that this hill I'm standing on...'

'Well, it didn't,' squeaked the boyo.

'It's been here only a year,' added the gal.

'A year and a half,' clarified the boyo.

'Yep,' conceded the gal.

'I see, it's the dirt from the pit they dug up for Carrefour... But where did those trees come from?' I pointed to the full-grown four-meter deciduous trees.

'Brought 'em in a truck, right,' explained the boyo patiently.

'Rolled out the grass, stuck in the trees, right, and that's that,' rasped the miss. The boyo sniffed uncertainly.

'That explains it then,' I said, again in a muted fashion, left them to carry on with their hanky-panky, and came to the railing.

I was standing on a brand-new hill overlooking Smíchov. Lights glittered in the clear darkness, so clear as to give one a headache. It wasn't snowing anymore. The glass pit of Anděl gleamed like a melting iceberg. Something rustled under my shoe. A newspaper someone had tossed out. I wiped off the dusting of snow. HUMAN ARM FOUND IN DUSTBIN, PRAGUE 6 announced the heading. A supermarket shopping centre the size of a residential block silently lounged below. Fresh wind was breaking apart the clouds above the city.

I was standing on a hill in pitch darkness. And suddenly it occurred to me that actually everything was perfectly in order here. Absolutely everything. That those tin ideals painted in screaming colours that for millennia people had died for, good, evil, the truth, this and that. That they're still here but fortunately no one takes them seriously anymore. Because every time these notions were publicly proffered, every time there was preaching about what's right and wrong, there was always someone with a bleeding nose and someone standing on a chair with a noose around their neck stiff from fear. It occurred to me that all it takes nowadays is to simply live honestly. And that there's no single reason to get upset over some insignificant details. That things have simply got as far as this and from here they will carry further. That it's not that we get what we deserve, but that things go through us and over us.

I was standing on a hill in pitch darkness between Kenvel and Carrefour; there was nowhere to step aside and no reason to step aside either. In paradise there was the rustling of paper and the sulking silence of the saints, while in hell the sweat of constantly screaming and screwing half-imbecile midgets sprayed all over; the stars were silent above and the roaring of lava resounded from below. I was standing on a heavy ship made of earth, full of cadavers engaged in lively conversation and squabbling, and the torn-up cob-webs of youth were flying from the mast.

And I was overwhelmed by an uncertain but unexpectedly strong feeling of happiness for living in exactly this time and no other, a time which is miraculous in that one can hear and experience and actually feel under one's feet this thundering blast with which it's all going to tear off with us any time now and descend again ever lower, somewhere downward, into the unknown.

Translated from the Czech by Petr Kopet

BERLIN

Something for Nothing

LARISSA BOEHNING

In early autumn the swallows leave the North. They criss-cross the sky in wide sweeping ribbons, drop away, dart side to side in the air, soar up again effortlessly, full of strength for the flight south. They only come back in the spring, fix their nests under the roof and live in these cracks during the year. You could follow the swallows' path along the dyke when they went south. They always flew over the land, never over the sea. When they went, you knew that autumn was coming. They take the light with them, someone once said. When they are gone, it gets dark.

He sold me his orangey-red Swallow moped. He said, 'one swallow doesn't make a summer', laughed as he said it. His face was broad, his beard stubbly and dense. He was wearing a dark blue cap. He introduced himself as Uli Fähnlein – 'Little Flag' – 'and I am the kind of person who's blowing in the wind, or something,' he laughed again. I thought, what a strange person with his sad laugh.

We went for a test drive through Neukölln, stopped by the bank, I took out 400DM. In front of his shop I counted it into his hand. It was windy, he laid his hand on mine and we ended up shaking hands.

'And if you need a camera', he said, pointing to his shop window, 'always come to me.' 'Why?' I asked, one foot on the starter, hands on the handlebars. 'I'll tell you that if you actually show up.'

On the day it happened I wheeled the Swallow out of the house and was just driving up the street, past the photo shop, when Uli called to me. I stopped, and he checked whether all the lights were working. 'It's not bad,' he said, 'it does sixty.' I nodded and drove off in the direction of the city centre.

The phone-call came in the early evening, I'd just come home. My mother couldn't stop crying, I couldn't ask her what had happened. I got on a train and went north. I arrived around midnight, a grey car was still standing in front of the house. 'They've already come for him,' my mother said as I came into the hallway, 'they just took him away.'

I didn't see my father again, just saw how he had left everything. His work-bench in his hobby room, the tweezers and the soldering iron lay around as if they had only just been put down, as if he would come back any moment and tidy everything away.

I stayed until the funeral. The morning after, my mother said, 'take the cameras away with you, I don't want the things here any more, they all stare at me.' I took them away with me, pulled the heavy bag across the station. My mother raised her hand and waved goodbye, I just asked her if she would cope with everything.

I put the bag with the cameras in out in the hall, I didn't want them in my room. The next morning I carried them over the road to the photo shop. Uli was sitting on a folding stool in front of the shop window, drinking coffee. 'Ah, well, well,' he said 'want something to drink?' He watched as I put the bag down and sat down next to him. 'What's happened here?' he asked, his gaze searched my face, he turned round to look at me. I told him about my father. 'Killed by smoking,' Uli said quietly, and shook his head, 'I'm sorry.' I sat there next to him, our arms were touching. I opened the bag and said, 'have a look.' He took them out one by one, turned over the cases, pressed the shutter release over and again, there was a metallic click in the cameras' insides. 'They're good,' Uli said appreciatively, 'did he collect them?' 'Yes,' I replied, 'haven't seen him take photos for years, he just put the things in the cabinet and took them out every now and then to clean them or to fiddle around with them.'

'I can't give you any money for them', Uli said, 'I'll have to sell some of them first.' I nodded. I didn't want to carry the bag any more and didn't want the lenses' empty eyes in my flat. 'Will you get rid of them?' I asked, and was immediately ashamed of the question. 'The Nikons are on a run just now,' Uli said, business-like, 'the Voigtländers are probably too old, no-one's buying that kind of thing just now, but all the Olympus stuff will go, I'm sure about that.'

He offered me some coffee, I shook my head. 'Don't you want to keep any of them?' he asked. A car revved loudly outside. 'I'll think about it,' I said, although I was sure I didn't want to have any of the cameras.

He looked at me for a moment. We were still sitting close to each other. I saw the large pores in the skin on his nose, his face. He had a very particular smell about him, part early-morning sleepiness, part cigarettes, and something old, maybe from the dust that was also lying around in the shop. He stood up, pushed the bag behind the counter, locked the door, hung a sign on it – 'SHORT BREAK!' – and sat down next to me again.

'Shall we go for a little walk?' he asked and pushed his cap back and forwards with a swift movement. I nodded.

'Let's take the Swallow,' he said, 'then we can go further out.'

We went into my yard, I picked up my helmet. 'The boss will drive today,' Uli said, levered the Swallow off its stand and pushed it out the yard. I got on behind him and held on around his waist. He was fat, his belly was firm. It was odd being so close to him. He was wearing a bobbly knitted jumper and a red scarf around his neck. He looked like a captain who no longer had a ship. He said, 'I'll show you something beautiful, kid.' As we set off I pressed myself closer to him. If anyone had asked, I would have said it was good, sitting behind him like that. Although I barely knew him. He just seemed like a friend, a confidant who'd just happened to come along.

We drove from Neukölln towards Kreuzberg, along the Landwehrkanal, drove once through Treptow Park. I signalled to him from behind 'keep going straight ahead,' he shook his head under the helmet. We parked at the foot of the Schlesische Brücke in front of an old petrol station. It was quiet, by comparison: I had got used to the loud noise of the engine. He pulled his helmet off his head, I carried on wearing mine. We walked over some factory grounds, through a rusty door and stood in an abandoned hall.

'Here's where we always used to practise,' he said.

'Practise what?' I asked.

'With our band,' Uli laughed, 'I'll show you the photos.'

'When?' I asked him, we went further into the hall, there was something in front of us not dissimilar to a steam locomotive. Next to it a puddle of rusty water. The smooth surface reflected the blind windows, the steel girders on the ceiling.

'Beginning of the nineties,' Uli said, 'just after the Wall came down, everything here has been abandoned since then.' We crossed the hall, water was dripping somewhere. Uli took my arm, 'come on, I'll show you something completely way-out.' We climbed up to the first floor via a narrow ladder. For a moment I was surprised that I was following him just like that.

We came into a room with steel lockers, the doors open and dented. A shoe was lying in one locker, as if someone might come and pick it up some time.

'It gets better,' Uli said. We walked past a washroom. The sinks stood in the middle like troughs, the mirrors on the wall were rusted away in patches. On a ledge lay a dirty chunk of soap.

'Someone's been here recently,' I said, and looked at Uli. He laughed. 'We'll soon see,' he whispered, 'come on.' I shoved my hands in my trouser pockets. I was still wearing my helmet. Uli pulled open an iron door. We came into a large room with rows of broad workbenches. Lying on top of them was a jumble of tools, metal, engine parts. It looked as if the workers had left everything standing or lying there when a bell sounded, home time, off, gone. I was silent. Uli reached for an oil-smeared hammer, 'that's a good tool,' he said, 'look here.' We walked between the rows of benches, Uli pocketed some tongs and a few screwdrivers. The air in the room was heavy, metallic and dusty.

'That's how a state comes to an end,' he said as he walked, 'deserted by everyone. Could have happened to us too, it happens so fast – you can see here just how fast it happens.' I nodded. Uli carried on walking through the rows. 'It's a nice image: the people simply leave everything behind, leave it all lying, in the factories, on the assembly lines, they don't go into the shops, there's no-one sitting at the tills, the buses and trains stay in the depots in the morning. I like that image,' he said quietly.

'What would you do,' I asked him, 'on a day like that?' He laughed. It was that serious laugh again, from someone who wears his despair just under the surface of his skin. 'I'd just sit in front of the shop, and watch the people in the street running from shop to shop, all of them shut or empty, no-one serving, and I'd watch them standing there not knowing what to do or where to go.' I grinned, took my helmet off, held it like a shopping basket and collected some work tools. 'So then you'd go shopping,' I shouted to him from one of the back rows, 'until there was nothing left.' 'And then,' Uli shouted back, 'we'd drive out to the allotments, go to Mum's, she's always got some potatoes spare.'

'Is there stuff here I could use for my moped?' I looked at him.

Uli had come over to me. He was gathering some smaller screwdrivers, shoving the tools to and fro on the bench with his fleshy hands.

'Take what you need,' I said. 'Yes, boss,' he laughed, 'that's called plundering a state.' 'What do you mean, a state,' I said, 'everything's just lying around here.'

'Maybe it's like a museum,' he grinned, 'do you take things from museums too?'

'That's different,' I said quickly. He had come right up to me, looked me right in the face.

'Sometimes you really like being a girl.'

'I don't have any other choice.' I turned away.

He moved off, propped himself against the doorframe with one hand. 'Our expedition carries on,' he said quietly, and turned to go. I cast another glance over the workbenches, I had the strange impression that the sounds of the work, the machines, still hung in the room. Uli called to me. I went to the workbench and grabbed a wrench. I moved the cold metal to and fro across the table. There were stubbed-out cigarette butts everywhere in the gaps. My father often used to rest his cigarette on the edge of the work-surface when he needed two hands. The smoke curled up in the air, the ash fell down to the ground. My mother used to sweep the workroom in the evening, conscientiously removing the remains of his work. I heard Uli calling to me again. I went into the stairwell, he was standing halfway up. 'Come on,' he said emphatically.

We walked through a corridor and came out onto an open balcony with a brick balustrade. In front of us was a waterway leading into the Spree.

'The border was here, over there was the West.' He pointed out the huge searchlights which were fixed to the roofs of the houses nearby. 'Was once a well guarded crossing.'

I leaned over the balustrade, saw the dark water of the canal. Rubbish and planks of wood were swimming along the narrow banks.

'It was all full of barbed wire round here until just recently,' he said slowly, 'someone or other started to remove it.' 'Safety reasons, probably,' he added, and laughed. 'They used to patrol up and down along this balcony.'

'Did anyone ever make it?' I asked, my belly still pressed up against the balustrade.

'I think so,' said Uli, 'I heard once that a man tried to swim across here.' He pushed himself off from the balustrade, wandered down the corridor. On the bank opposite I could see an allotment site, with squat sheds, brightly coloured umbrellas, a jetty where small boats were tied up.

'Looks like a peaceful life over there', I said as Uli came back and stood next to me.

'But not exactly my dream destination either,' he said.

'If you could just go away somewhere, where would you go?' I asked him suddenly. He picked up his helmet.

'Greece, one of the islands,' he said quickly, 'I went there once to a small house in the mountains. From the top you had a clear view of the sea.'

'Why don't you do it?' I asked. He reached for a screw which was lying on the balustrade and threw it far into the Spree. 'Let's go. I want to show you something else.'

Carrying our helmets like baskets, we went down the

fire-escape stairs to the floor below. We were back in the corridor which seemed to run along the building on the side nearest the Spree. Through the bars of the railing I could see the other river bank. It smelled of urine and stagnant water. 'I'd like to introduce you to someone,' Uli said, and went on ahead.

At the end of the corridor a steel door stood ajar. Uli disappeared, I followed him. It led into a high, square room, canvases, stone sculptures and figures made of bits of iron welded together everywhere. Uli shouted, 'Come here, kid.' I was annoyed that he was calling me that here.

'Wolfgang, what's up?' Uli asked in a loud voice. 'Hey,' said Wolfgang, and carried on rolling his cigarette. His greasy hat had slipped down his neck. His face was grey as dust. He screwed his eyes up and looked at me. His eyebrows were broad, a few hairs stood out like spiders' legs. Uli was talking as if he had to talk for three. Wolfgang lit the crumpled cigarette behind a cupped hand, the room smelled of petrol and dust. I looked around, and put my helmet down, even though I wanted to go. 'Uli,' I began. 'What are you doing here?' interrupted Wolfgang and looked at Uli. 'Just wanted to see if you're still alive,' he answered. 'Thanks for that,' said Wolfgang. Uli looked uncertain, looked around, looked at me. A door banged and a woman came from the back of the room. Her long dark blond hair hung down her like two stripes. 'That's Inge,' Uli said to me.

'I'm Inge,' the woman repeated, once she was standing next to me. She was very thin, and had no bust whatsoever. Wolfgang was smoking, Uli swung his helmet and let it knock against his legs. The tools inside knocked against each other and made metallic noises.

'Did you get those upstairs?' Inge asked.

'Yes,' I said quickly, and saw that she was scrutinising my helmet. 'So you've gone and taken the best bits,' Inge said. Her voice was sharp and strangely hollow.

'Okay you two,' Uli said, 'we've got to head off.' I nodded to Inge. 'Yeah, hey,' Wolfgang called after us.

Outside Uli caught my gaze. 'He's lost his sense of humour,' he said. It was more a question. I said, 'no wonder, with a girlfriend like that.' Uli laughed briefly. 'Come on, kid, let's get back.' For a brief second I wondered why he kept calling me that.

He stopped the Swallow in front of the shop, put the stand down. I stood on the pavement, the pockets in my jacket hung low with the tools in. 'What are you up to tonight?' he asked, trying to be casual. I took everything out of my pockets, saw that my hands were smeared with dirt and said 'I've got plans already.' He unlocked the door, took the tools out of my hands and went inside. 'Are they staying here?' I asked. He said, 'if the Swallow breaks down it'll be me who repairs it anyway.' 'Okay,' I drawled, 'I'll remind you of that when the time comes.' Uli had disappeared into the cellar. I stood there, uncertain. Everywhere I looked there was stuff, cameras, cine-cameras, magazines, old leather photo bags. The wall behind the sales counter was covered in photos. I recognised Uli on them. One picture showed five lads in green light, a band, the singer was jumping up with his legs wide, leaning on the mike stand. In the background a man was hanging from the ceiling on a rope like a cocoon, upside down. I heard Uli coming up the steps. 'Was that you?' I asked. Uli's gaze followed where my finger was pointing. 'Yes, that was us. I'm the one at the back.'

'What,' I laughed, 'the one hanging?'

'No, that's not me,' said Uli, 'that's Wolfgang, I'm the one here.' He pointed to the jumping singer. 'We used to do the music for his happenings. Was a fun time.' He went out the back again, I heard a cassette recorder clattering as a tape was put in. The music filled the shop. Uli stood in the hallway, looked at me and grinned.

I drove the Swallow into town to work, but not up our street, not past the photo shop. On Saturday morning I found a note in my letterbox, saying 'You haven't exactly won the lottery, but I've sold two Nikons. Come over, Uli.'

I went to the photo shop, sat myself down on the folding stool which stood outside, and waited until Uli finished serving all the customers. 'Alright, kid,' he greeted me. I was glad that he didn't seem to mean anything by it. We drank some coffee. In the pub across the street a woman had a go at a man. A girl walked past, pulling her dog behind her, right in front of us he pissed against a tree.

'And, what have you been up to?' Uli asked. I wondered what I ought to tell him. He stood up suddenly, went into the shop. I thought, does he want to hear or not. 'Sorry,' he said, when he came back out again, 'you can start now.' I said nothing.

From across the street a little man came towards us. 'Fähnlein,' the figure shouted and grinned, 'leave the women alone.' 'I haven't done anything,' shouted Uli, holding up his hands. 'That's Hoffmann,' he said to me, and when Hoffmann was standing in front of him, 'Hi, how's it going today?'

'It's going,' said Hoffmann, 'it's going.' He was wearing a greasy suit which had got too big for him, the trousers were held together by a belt with a buckle. 'Got anything for me?' Hoffmann asked, 'I might have some spare capacity.' He pronounced *capacity* slowly and clearly, as if he had just learnt the word and wanted to try out how it sounded.

'Yeah, I've got some stuff lying around here,' Uli said, went into the shop and returned with two old cameras. 'These belong to the lady here,' Uli said. 'This one has something wrong with the shutter release. And on this one the catch sticks sometimes.'

'Fine, fine,' said Hoffmann, 'that can be sorted.'

As he went, I said to Uli, 'I can't believe they're broken, my father would definitely have repaired them.'

'They aren't broken,' said Uli, and raised his coffee cup. 'But Hoffmann needs something to do. Otherwise he'll just think about the fact that it will all be over soon.' I was silent.

'You work and work and then you fall off your stool,' Uli said, and laughed his sad laugh, 'what else is there.'

'Hm, whatever comes in between,' I said.

A customer went into the shop, Uli followed, and I stayed where I was. When he came out again, he said, 'I'm taking photos at a kind of art thing this evening. One of Wolfgang's. If you fancy it, you could come along too.'

We drove there on the Swallow. Uli didn't talk much, I was quiet too, there was something cold about him. I couldn't have said what. I followed him across the car park. The light from a couple of street lamps was reflected in the expanse of puddle surfaces. It was part of the factory grounds that we'd been in a while ago. We climbed down a narrow ladder and stood with our heads tucked in under the arches of the ceiling. Uli nodded to me. I lost myself among the crowd. The room slowly filled up, we stood under the low ceiling and breathed in the smell of the damp plasterwork.

Inge came over to me. 'I know you,' she said, 'you're Uli's girlfriend aren't you?' I shook my head, was going to say that I wasn't his girlfriend, just a friend, and said 'yes.'

She came and stood right up close to me. I moved away a bit.

'He's a good bloke,' Inge said loudly, 'I can see that. Just a bit fat.' I thought of dusty Wolfgang, his sinuous, almost gouty hands, which had lit the cigarette, and said 'I don't think so.'

'Nah, course not,' Inge said, 'love makes you blind. I'm like that too.'

I said nothing.

'Do you know Uli married a friend of mine?' Inge looked at me searchingly.

'No, I didn't know,' I said, and tried to look uninterested.

'Yeah well, it's a while ago now,' she said, 'and it really was an emergency.'

I couldn't help it, and looked questioningly at her.

'It was before the Wall came down,' she remarked. On the stage in front a lump of meat slapped to the floor. Blood spurted. 'A friend of mine, she was pregnant, and wanted to leave for the West. So he married her. She claimed that the child was his.'

'And was it?' I asked.

'No idea. You don't know what goes on in other people's beds,' Inge said, and looked at me. Her lips were narrow, and her make-up went over the edges. She was wearing a smock with deep cut-out armholes, and no bra underneath. At the front something slapped again, a floppy, wet sound.

'You can ask him about it,' she said, 'but I don't think he likes talking about it.'

It struck me that Uli wore a broad gold ring, which almost seemed to have grown into his finger, I had noticed it the very first time we met, when I had bought the Swallow. It looked antique. I had thought then that he was wearing his parents' old wedding ring.

'He looked after her well,' Inge said. 'That's what my friend always said.' She said it with a tone of appreciation, but also complicity: I know more than you, I know other things that you don't know about, and if you ask me I might tell you. But I didn't fancy asking her, I said, 'I need to go get something to drink.'

I found Uli at the back of the room. He was leaning against a wall, one leg bent, and was putting a film in the camera. 'Kid,' he said, 'is this your kind of thing?' He put his hand on my arm, and said, 'have you seen, Inge is here, that's someone you know already, even if she's not someone you like talking to.'

'It's okay,' I said, 'we've already said hello.'

'Ah,' said Uli, and looked at me. 'Wolfgang with his meat, it's mad, isn't it?'

I nodded and drank.

'But I've taken a couple of fun photos, some real slabs with loads of blood.'

'It smells really strong in here,' I said quietly, as Uli turned away. He went back to the stage, I stood where I was, and looked at the backs of the people in front of me. I had wanted to ask him if it had really been like that.

Later, as he came over to me, he asked, 'do you want to stay or go?' His voice was deep, heavy with beer, the camera lens pressed against my hip as he leant towards me.

'I want to go,' I said quickly, 'but I don't want to go home.'

'Enough meat for today,' Uli said, and led the way up the small ladder.

The night was lukewarm, a clear sky and no wind. We sat down on the edge of the kerb, stretched out our legs, and both of us looked straight ahead.

'That was it, once,' Uli said then, 'but it's over. You can't get it back.'

I thought of Inge, her boney breast, her over–lipsticked mouth, which opened and shut silently. In a strange way I'd got a bit of a fright when he said it was over. He was silent, I asked, 'what?' and looked at him from the side.

'The time when I used to think that was good. That something like that was good.'

'Dropping meat?'

'Yes, everything, the whole fuss and nonsense. It isn't what matters. None of it is what actually matters.'

Two women walked past us across the car park and laughed loudly. I lay down on my back on the pavement, Uli scrutinised me from above. I folded my hands across my stomach.

'You're lying in the dirt, kid,' Uli said slowly. 'Doesn't matter,' I said.

'Doesn't matter, nothing matters,' Uli said and laughed scornfully. 'I'd love to run through the city at night, screaming, nothing matters! Wake everyone up out of their dreams and scream, do you hear me, you idiots, nothing matters!'

'I'm with you,' I said. He looked at me, astonished. I sat up, rubbed my hands and said it again, 'come on, let's go.'

We got onto the Swallow, raced over the cobblestones back to Neukölln and screamed above the sound of the engine for the whole journey. We drove through the night, the smell of the two-stroke in our noses, and I held on tight to Uli's waist, leaned back and screamed. Uli leaned forwards, into the headwind, and screamed louder than me. We were an Ascension Day commando. We were drunk.

It was a while before we saw each other again. My Swallow wouldn't start and I wheeled it out the yard, across the street over to the photo shop. Uli wasn't there, the sign was hanging on the door and I thought, then I'll wait.

He came round the corner, out of Sonnenallee. He was holding an ice-cream in front of him, a few scoops in a tub. When he was standing in front of me, he pulled the light blue paper umbrella out of the ice-cream and threw it on the road.

'I've always loved those,' I said. He bent down slowly and picked it up. 'Here,' he said, 'it's for you. If I'd known you were going to show up, I'd have brought you an ice-cream.'

I unfurled the umbrella, ran my finger carefully over the paper, thin as silk, and twirled it between my thumb and forefinger.

'Something up with the Swallow?' he said, as he walked into the shop. I followed him.

'It won't start.'

He repeated the sentence, drawing out the words, turned round to face me and said, 'well I guess Uli Fähnlein will have to repair it then.'

I didn't say anything, just looked at him. I was about to say, you're the one with the tools, but kept quiet instead. He went behind the counter, tidied some money away into the till, sorted out some receipts, then said suddenly, 'the girl only comes round when she wants something. And when you aren't expecting her any more.'

I shoved my hands in my trouser pockets and stood in the door with my stomach sticking out. 'You said you would repair it.' Uli looked at me for a moment. 'But not today,' he said, 'today I need some peace and quiet for once'.

I tried to smile, he walked past me.

'I'm going back down the cellar,' he said, 'I can get some peace there.'

He bent down under the counter, rummaged in a chest. He seemed to be looking for something.

'Another time then, I'll leave the Swallow here,' I said quietly, and opened the door, making the little bells chime.

'Where are you going?' he called after me.

'Home,' I said without turning round. It was only when I was back in my flat that I realised I'd left the light blue paper umbrella lying on the counter.

The summer spread out over the city, the dry air turned dusty. The streets smelled of dogs and pre-cooked meals. I left the window open, even at night, the summer stole into the flat from outside and made it a part of the city. It was evening, already late, when the doorbell rang. Uli was standing in the dark hallway, casually leaning his shoulder against the wall. He grinned, and asked, 'shall we have a drink?' I let him in, he rummaged in his shoulder bag and produced an old camera. 'What am I meant to do with that?' I asked him. He said, 'cleaned up by Hoffmann, it's a good piece, keep it. I can't sell it anyway.' I took the camera and didn't know what to do with it. I put it in the kitchen. Uli followed me. He pulled two beer bottles from his bag.

We had been sitting quite a while at the table in the kitchen when suddenly a loud wail, like singing, came from the yard.

'Neukölln's a great place to live,' Uli said, and didn't laugh. I went into the bedroom, where you can look out over the whole yard. I saw a man lying on his back in front of the dustbins, surrounded by three women. Uli came over to me at the window. I stepped back a bit. 'Well,' he said, 'he's had it.' 'You're kidding,' I whispered. 'He's dead,' Uli said matter-of-factly.

I closed the window quietly and carefully. The yard was lit by two bare lightbulbs. In the pale light the women knelt down and stood up again, they sang, they beat their hands in front of their faces. I leant against the pane, and noticed Uli coming up behind me. 'He's just fallen over there,' I said. 'Kid,' Uli shouted, 'he's stone dead.'

'How undignified,' I said quietly, 'you don't die in front of the rubbish bins in a filthy yard like this.' 'Dying is always undignified,' Uli said, 'and in any case, you never know where it'll get you.' The singing echoed between the walls, one woman kept smoothing the man's hair out of his eyes. She rocked her torso slowly back and forth.

After a while paramedics rushed into the yard, followed by a younger woman, they knelt down in front of the man. Their jackets glowed in the light from the lightbulbs. The women's singing died away. I moved away from the window, my back bumped against Uli's stomach. He put his hands on my hips. 'Maybe,' he said quietly, 'there's a small chance in this case.'

The paramedics put the man on a stretcher, covered him with a blanket up to his chin, and carried him out. Uli was still standing behind me. Lights had now come on in some of the windows of the houses opposite. Shadow figures gathered in the crossbars of the windows. 'Maybe,' I said and pulled away from Uli's hands. We stood facing each other. He looked at me for a long time. I looked down.

'Should I stay,' he asked quietly, 'or should I go?'

'Don't mind,' I said. He hesitated, walked around the room, unsure, picked up his jacket, held it in his hands. 'Stay,' I said, and left the room, I wanted to be as far away from the yard as possible.

He came after me, stood in the hall and said 'Marie.' He said my name like it was a statement and at the same time a curse. He just stood there and said, 'Marie'. I went back into the room, lay down on my front on the sofa, and breathed into the cushions. I stayed lying like that, and fell asleep at some point.

I woke up, not for long, and didn't know how long I'd been asleep. I noticed that Uli was sitting next to me on the sofa, his hand was resting on my neck, his fingers were touching my skin. I opened my eyes just a crack. It was dark in the room, I could smell the unwashed fuzz of his jumper.

I stayed where I was on the sofa. In the early morning I woke up with an aching back and went to lie down in bed. Uli was fully dressed, and turned to face the wall when I got under the covers. We didn't touch. We got up around midday, and I looked out the window onto the yard. It looked the same as always, dirty around the rubbish bins, straggly bushes behind them.

'Well?' asked Uli.

'I might have just been dreaming,' I answered.

He said as he went, 'come by the shop, if you fancy. For the Swallow, too.'

I said I'd think about it. Maybe I'd go away. 'Where?' he asked, astonished.

'I don't know,' I said, 'just away.'

He looked back up the stairwell once, as if he wanted to

capture an image of me. He raised his hand briefly. It was a strangely half-hearted, incomplete gesture.

It was only later, much later, that I recalled that my father had once said: don't ever wait for the swallows, they only come when you're no longer expecting them. It had been in the spring, on the dyke, I remember. Once, sometime in the winter, I had found a swallow's nest in the garden. It had fallen down, was just lying there among the thatch which dropped out of the roof. I had shown it to my mother and then put it in the shed. At the end of the winter I'd driven out to the dyke and had thrown it far out into the creek. I waited for a while, but it didn't resurface.

Translated from the German by Lyn Marven

AMSTERDAM

My Mother's Men

ARNON GRUNBERG

On Friday nights, my mother hosts single men. The oldest is ninety-four, the youngest is in his fifties. Some of them only come for the food; others hope for more.

My mother was offered several men after my father had died but she prefers to stick to her Friday-evening routine.

Occasionally, one of them has managed to get to sleep over. My mother, a cautious woman by nature, would carefully lock her bedroom door. This didn't always work, however. Once she had a bear of a man staying over (this was her description of him) — even though I had told her that she shouldn't invite anyone who looks like a bear in the first place. In the middle of the night, she heard someone banging on her bedroom door. My mother, who thinks you should always consider the worst-case scenario first, thought there was a fire or a burglar. But it was only the bear in pyjamas standing at her bedroom door and muttering, 'I want to talk to you about your son.'

'Surely not in the middle of the night?' my mother answered.

That put an end to the sleepover parties.

'I'm not running a hotel!' she told me. 'Besides, he's always trying to press his dirty mouth onto my lips. And he eats like an animal.'

My mother thinks mouths are dirty in general, and she keeps an accurate account of her visitors' eating habits. She calls me sometimes and says, 'Mister X didn't touch his half chicken,' or, 'Mister Y spent an hour on the toilet again. His bowel movements are getting more and more difficult.'

Nothing gets past her, and I am kept fully up to date. 'Maybe you can use it in your writing,' she sometimes adds, prompted by her unvanquishable fear of her son ending up as a bagman under a bridge. She considers it her maternal duty to provide me with material. That way, we can join forces and push ourselves further away from the poverty line. 'People say you get that from me,' she says.

My mother refers to anyone who isn't a relative of hers as 'people.'

'Quick,' she used to say, 'People are coming. Clean everything up.'

Her own relatives are apparently somewhere on the periphery of the human race and my mother saw herself as a barely disguised subversive entity.

My mother wanted her children to become acquainted with her men, and to that end, she invited us to Amsterdam. My mother's men, each in his own way, are also somewhere on the periphery of the human race. That was not the reason, however, for my hesitation in accepting the invitation. I don't mind seeing the occasional relative, but all of them at once is asking too much.

I arrived in Amsterdam with trepidation. Perhaps it was better not to get acquainted with my mother's men. There is no need to know everything. It is better if you don't. Besides, my sister was going to be there.

My sister lives in a settlement on the West Bank, has six children, wears tent dresses and strange hats. Her husband knows a lot about God, his beard is old and his eyes are fierce. My oldest cousins see in me the sinner that I may very well be.

I greeted my relatives and went to great lengths to become a relative myself. I took a baby in my lap and tossed it into the air a couple of times.

'Be careful,' my mother cried, 'it will fall on the floor.'

But it didn't fall on the floor.

'Don't worry,' I said, 'she has six of them.'

My mother, too, feels a certain distance towards her grandchildren. 'I can't help it,' she remarked about one of them, 'but he makes me puke.' There is no doubt, however, that she loves her grandson. You can love even those who make you puke. Even I have made people puke, and yet I have never been at a loss for love.

'How is it possible,' I asked my mother, 'that you had two such crazy children? One takes God's word literally, the other takes his own words literally. One treats the world like a ritual bath house, the other like a bazaar filled with flea market junk. One thinks love comes from God, the other that love is a bargaining chip. It may very well be that your children have watered and fertilized the seeds of insanity, but couldn't it be true that you and dad planted those seeds?'

My mother wouldn't hear of the seeds of insanity. 'There is no such thing in our family.'

And my sister says, 'There's nothing wrong with me — you're the one who's bananas.'

So we both think the other one's crazy, and that creates a bond as well.

On Thursday night, my mother began cooking for her men; reservations were made for the senior citizen's taxi service. Not all of the guests were particularly mobile anymore.

I tried very hard to come up with an excuse for getting out of the Friday night appointment, but my guilt got the better of me. And so I arrived at my parental home well on time. My mother was running back and forth between the kitchen and the living room, my sister was reciting prayers, and I was pacing around the garden. One by one, my mother's men arrived, some of them on foot, some of them by bicycle, and a few via the senior citizen's taxi service.

'Why don't you go and talk to the guests while I finish the potato salad?' my mother said.

It's not being that is unbearably light — it's despair. Like a balloon, the despair rose and hovered against the ceiling.

I barely managed to keep one conversation going. It was about haemorrhoids. My contribution was: 'Haemorrhoids are just like tonsils: you take them out with scissors.' Apparently my mother liked men with haemorrhoids (everyone looks for his own periphery). I was playing the role of my mother's son, but I'd had better days.

Dinner was served, and my mother ran like an athlete, for fear her men might leave her home hungry.

'So,' one of her men said, 'now the family is complete?'

Even if we were a family, it was quite an experimental one.

My mother cut the meat. 'I bought a new shower head especially for him,' she called out, 'he likes a hard spray.' The men turned their attention to me. Well, well, I could hear them thinking, the writer likes a hard spray. I shrank further and further, but there was no emergency exit here. I had to play family member for a little while longer.

'I like a hard spray too,' said the youngest of my mother's men, 'but the water pressure in Amsterdam isn't good enough. There's no use getting a new shower head.'

'This one has three settings,' my mother answered, serving generous portions of meat. 'You should all come up and see for yourselves after dinner.'

After dinner, those assembled indeed climbed the stairs to admire my mother's shower head.

At the bottom of the stairs, my mother whispered to me, 'Be nice to Mister Z, will you, he's on death's doorstep.'

Even the dying expressed an interest in shower heads.

Nothing surprised me anymore; all I longed for was to get off the stage and into the dressing room where I could remove my make-up.

And as my mother demonstrated the hard spray of her shower head, I wondered why we dare not choose happiness for ourselves, why, instead, we do everything to run away from it, in order not to risk losing it again.

Translated from the Dutch by
Lisa Friedman and Ron de Klerk.

Contributors

Larissa Boehning was born in Berlin in 1971. Her debut collection, *Schwalbensommer* (Swallow Summer, 2003), received critical acclaim, firmly establishing her as one to watch.

David Constantine is an award–winning poet and translator. His volumes of poetry include *Madder, Watching for Dolphins, The Pelt of Wasps, Something for the Ghosts* and the epic poem *Casper Hauser*. He is a translator of Hölderlin, Brecht, Goethe, Kleist, Enzensberger, Michaux and Joccottet. In 2003 he was shortlisted for the Whitbread Poetry Prize and in the same year won the Corneliu M Popescu Prize for European Poetry in Translation. In 2004 his poem 'Trilobite in Wenlock Shales' was shortlisted for Best Individual Poem in the Forward Prize. His second collection of short stories, *Under The Dam* was published in 2005.

Born in 1971 in Amsterdam **Arnon Grunberg** is one of the most widely read young European writers today. After he had been kicked out of high school, he worked as assistant in a drugstore, as dishwasher, publisher, and playwright for an Amsterdam theater company. In 1994, at 23, he made his debut with the internationally acclaimed novel *Blue Mondays* which won him two awards: for the best and for the bestselling debut novel.

Emil Hakl (aka Jan Beneš) was born in Prague in 1958. After graduating from the Jaroslav Jezek Conservatorium, he worked as a copywriter and as the editor of the literary magazine *Tvar*. In the late 80s, Hakl founded an informal literary group called Moderní analfabet. Hakl made his literary debut with two collections of poetry, followed shortly by a collection of stories *Konec sveta* (2001). Since then Hakl has written a novel , *Intimní schránka Sabriny Black* (2002), a novella *O rodicích a detech* (2002), and a second collection of stories *O létajících objektech* (2004). *O rodicích a detech* (2002) won the distinguished Magnesia Litera Prize and is currently being turned into a film.

Amanda Michalopoulou was born in Athens in 1966 and belongs to the youngest generation of Greek novelists. She has published a collection of short stories *Outside Life Is Colourful* and has contributed to several anthologies. Her first novel *Wishbone Memories* was awarded the 1996 novel prize of the literary magazine Diavazo. Her latest *How Many Times Can You Bear It*, taking its title from Kafka´s journals, is the story of a middle-aged Greek woman pursuing her Czech lover across Europe, a parody of road novels, stories of unhappy love and tales of the supernatural.

Empar Moliner burst onto the Catalan and Spanish literary scene in 1999 with her book, *L' ensenyador de pisos que odiava els mims*, a collection of satirical stories demonstrating a cold, sarcastic, and sometimes shocking view of everyday obsession. Her first novel, *Feli, esthéticienne*, is a comic account of passion; it was awarded the prominent Josep Pla Prize in 2000. Her collection of stories, *T'estimo si he begut,* was awarded the most influential Catalan literary prize, the Lletra d'Or Prize, and was voted the book of the year by *La Vanguardia* and *El Periódico* magazines. She currently works as a writer and journalist.

Aldo Nove, real name Antonello Satta Centanin, lives in Milan, translates from English, works for several daily papers and writes lyrics for the rock band Democrazia Cristiana and the musician, Garbo. His first story collection *Woobinda e altre storie senza lieto fine* (Woobinda and Other Stories Without A Happy Ending) was published in 1996 and two years later the extended version was published under the title *Superwoobinda*. His novels are *Puerto Plata market* (1997) and *Amore mio infinito* (My Immortal Beloved, 2000).

Jacques Réda is best known for his verse and prose explorations of urban and suburban landscapes, on foot, bicycle or Solex. He is a jazz critic and editor (he was at the head of the *Nouvelle Revue Française* from 1987 to 1997). His poetry collections include *Récitatif* and *La Tourne*, whilst his prose works include *The Ruins of Paris*, published in English in 1996, and the collection of short stories *La Liberté des Rues*.

Dalibor Šimpraga (b. 1969) is a writer and editor of the weekly magazine *Globus. Kavice Andreja Puplina* (Andrej Puplin's Coffee Chats), a collection of short stories about the lives of 20-year-olds living in the 90's in Zagreb, was published in 2002. These tales of the urban, everyday life of a lost war generation were originally published on the internet, and came into publication through popular demand. Director Branko Ištvancic has since adapted them for cinema, and the actor Hrvoje Zalar has dramatised them for the stage. Together with the writer Igor Štiks, Šimpraga edited the Anthology of new Croatian prose fiction from the 90's, *22 u hladu* (22 in the Shade, 1999).

Ágúst Borgþór Sverrisson's first stories were published in his high school magazine, and in 1987 his story 'Saknaa' (Missing) appeared in the Icelandic literary magazine *TMM*. At the time he was working on his first short story collection, and the poetry book *Eftirlast augnablik* (Wanted Moments). To date, Sverrisson has published five collections of short stories, the latest being *Tvisvar Ã Ãvinni* (Twice in a Lifetime, 2004). His stories have also appeared in numerous magazines. He is working on his first novel.

Special Thanks

This project has been realised only through the support, encouragement and expertise of a wide range of people, many of them volunteering their time to research, read and translate potential contributions. Among the 'without whoms' are:

Roman Simic, Teresa Halikowska–Smith, Gordana 'Goga' Matic, Snjezana Husic, Alexandra Büchler, Ana Makek, Sharon Keighley, Morana Peric, Christine Kessler, Ivana Kordic, Vera Juliusdottir, Mirjana 'Piki' Cibulka, Zoe Lambert, Isaac Shaffer, Sara D'Orazio, Olga Šunyara, Isabelle Croissant, Karen Leeder, Suzie Troup, Hans Gunnarson, Jon Yngvi, Anastasia Valassopoulos, Richard Crossan, Petr Gunter, Alannah Gunter, Tim Parks, Jette Howard, Kate Griffin, Diana Reich, Faith Liddell, Helen Constantine, Tuyet Ramzy, Matthew Crossan, Beverley Hoyle, Jean Laurie, and Karen Reppin for her help in editing the Emil Hakl translation. Not to mention the writers and translators themselves who have all gone out of their way in their contribution to this project.

Thanks are also due to Dave Eckersall for his saint-like patience with design illiterates, and of course the tireless Comma crew who during this period included: Sarah Eyre, Tom Spooner, Yvonne Sewell, Helen Raymond, Colin Jones, Raychel Higgs, and most especially Jim Hinks, for his stoicism and unerring enthusiasm.

ALSO AVAILABLE FROM COMMA...

Under the Dam
and other stories

DAVID CONSTANTINE

ISBN 0954828011
RRP: £7.95

'Flawless and unsettling'
Boyd Tonkin, Books of the Year, *The Independent*

'I started reading these stories quietly, and then became obsessed, read them all fast, and started re-reading them again and again. They are gripping tales, but what is startling is the quality of the writing. Every sentence is both unpredictable and exactly what it should be. Reading them is a series of short shocks of (agreeably envious) pleasure.'
- A S Byatt, Book of the Week, *The Guardian*

'A superb collection'- *The Independent*

'This is a haunting collection filled with delicate clarity. Constantine has a sure grasp of the fear and fragility within his characters.'
- A L Kennedy

ALSO AVAILABLE FROM COMMA...

The Book of Leeds
A CITY IN SHORT FICTION

Edited by Maria Crossan & Tom Palmer

ISBN 1-905583-01-X
EAN 978-1-905583-01-0
RRP: £7.95

Featuring:
Tony Harrison, Jeremy Dyson, Shamshad Khan, Ian Duhig, David Peace, Susan Everett, M.Y. Alam, Andrea Semple, Martyn Bedford and Tom Palmer.

The Book of Leeds is anthology of ten short stories, set in and around the city streets. The book reflects the quality and breadth of writing by contemporary Leeds authors, as work by acclaimed short story writers, poets, novelists and screenwriters are brought together in a ficitonal exploration of the city.

The book includes stories set in each decade of the last fifty years, stories that detail how Leeds has evolved from a postwar city falling into decline after the demise of the textile trade, into a successful modern city, with both problems and promise. They are about how the people of Leeds have come to terms with these changes and challenges, and continue to do so.

Ellipsis #1
comma modern shorts

sean o'brien
tim cooke
jean sprackland

ISBN 0-9548280-2-X
RRP: £7.95

An out-of-season seaside town, a library stocked with memories, a man slowly going mad...

Starting in the hotels and suburbs of a down-at-heel coastal town, Jean Sprackland's stories follow a cast of rootless characters, young men and women clinging to tokens of the past, whose lives are so lacking in ballast they become as unstable as the dunes themselves.

Tim Cooke invites us into a very different space: the derelict rooms and vandalised stairwells of an inner city tower-block. From there, each story draws a claustrophobic spiral round the next, following various characters (or is it the same person?) desperate to flee their demons.

Sean O'Brien's stories also spiral outwards - not from a state of mind but a setting: an ornate, vaulted lending library, an edifice from another age, where unlikely users and chance items found in stock lead to quite different lamentations for the past.

"Sprackland's stories combine narrative energy with affecting compassion for her troubled characters... she has now arrived as a short story writer. Tim Cooke is another extremely exciting author...bold...and skilled."
- Time Out

Ellipsis #2
comma modern shorts

jane rogers
polly clark
zoe lambert

ISBN 0 9548280 3 8
EAN 978 0 9548280 3 5
RRP: £7.95

A bank manager arrives at work one day to find himself the new employer of his ex-wife.

In the middle of a shift a divorced bus driver abandons his vehicle, to search for his estranged son.

Two sisters come to terms with their father's disappearance with the help of a skeleton called Indira.

The stories in *Ellipsis 2* explore the inherent dysfunctionality of almost all relationships, their aftermaths, and the lengths people go to to redeem them. From the ingrained resentments of Jane Rogers' parent-child histories, to the twisted claustrophobia of Polly Clark's couples, and the absence that travels beside each passenger in Zoe Lambert's bus sequence – these stories demonstrate the transforming, often alienating effect a relationship can have on the individuals in it, and remind us that being next of kin isn't always kind.

Ellipsis is a unique series presenting linked or themed sequences of short stories by three writers in each volume. All three are previously uncollected as short story authors, two of them in each issue are established (as novelists or poets), the third, in this case Zoe Lambert, is previously unpublished.